& THE
STREET KIDS

LUCY MOORE

Scripture Union

Copyright © Lucy Moore 2002

First published 2002

Scripture Union, 207–209 Queensway, Bletchley, Milton Keynes,
MK2 2EB, England.
Email: info@scriptureunion.org.uk
Website: www.scriptureunion.org.uk

ISBN 1 85999 566 7

British Library Cataloguing-in-Publication Data.
A catalogue record of this book is available from the British
Library.

Printed and bound in Great Britain by Cox & Wyman Ltd,
Reading, Berkshire.

*Scripture Union is an international Christian charity working with
churches in more than 130 countries, providing resources to bring
the good news about Jesus Christ to children, young people and
families and to encourage them to develop spiritually through the
Bible and prayer.*

*As well as our network of volunteers, staff and associates who run
holidays, church-based events and school Christian groups, we
produce a wide range of publications and support those who use
our resources through training programmes.*

For Rosie and Debbie King with much love

1

It was dark in the street and Chico tripped over the body.

'Hey! Marco! Take a look at this!' he breathed.

I pushed him to one side, but gently, because Chico only comes up to the neck of my T-shirt and is better than a blood-brother to me. I only had a second to see it was a man lying in the gutter before Luiz had shouldered his way in front of me.

'Push off, Marco,' he growled, and crouched over the figure in the gutter. He gave a hiss of satisfaction. 'Hey, a foreigner! Loaded by the look of his suit. Bit late for you to be out on our patch, mister. Maybe I'll just have a feel in your pocket...'

In the shadows we saw him stretch out a hand into the man's jacket, but before he could take anything, the man lashed out and Luiz jumped back with a gasp of pain. His eyes narrowed and his features tensed into the look he has sometimes of a cornered rat – the sort you turn and run from when you meet them in the sewers. Luiz whipped out his knife, a sliver of silvery steel in the palm of his hand. In a silent reflex action, the gang surrounded the man, blades pointing down towards him. On the streets you act quicker than you think.

We weighed the weapons in our hands, staring down at the helpless adult at our feet.

Suddenly I hated this. I hated the razor-sharp blade I held, I hated the fear we could smell pouring out of the man. I hated the darkness of the streets that forced us to assume we were in danger with the flicker of every shadow.

But Luiz loved it. He loved to see other people in his power.

The man looked up and caught my eye. His face was tired with a weariness that comes from a long time of being afraid. He looked me straight in the eye and I knew my disloyalty to the gang was showing in the pity I felt for him. His face twisted in a half-smile and he looked away.

Luiz spoke now, a low stream of curses and threats, crouching down lower and lower over the man. I found myself squatting down over him too, ready now either to protect the little ones from the man, or to protect the man from Luiz.

Luiz hissed his last mouthful of slime that I would not have had Bebe and the others hear. Then his wrist flicked up in the practised jerk of a slasher: I had seen the routine before – three or four flicks then a sharp jabbing slice downwards and the man would carry a scar on his face for the rest of his life, however long or short that was.

Luiz flicked once, twice – I tensed to intercept the blow. Three—

'*Stop!*' The voice came from behind me. I whirled round in relief. Luiz swore with frustration and tried to hide the knife.

'How many times must I tell you? *We do not rob!*'

Maria didn't have to push her way through the gang as we stood there, not sure what would happen next. The kids parted to let her through and she strode forward to stand over the silent man. He was hunched in on himself now, one hand over his head, the other clutching his ankle.

Then he looked up and for the first time I could see in the moonlight that there was more than fear in his eyes: he was in pain too. But I kept quiet. The long silent moment seemed to stretch into minutes as the two of them confronted each other.

'Your foot's bust,' said Maria at last.

'What? "Bust"?'

'Your foot hurts,' Maria translated.

'I fell and hurt it. It's nothing.'

'Is that why you don't scarper... run away?'

'I have nothing to steal,' the man said with great weariness and great dignity, considering he was lying in the gutter at our feet. 'A pickpocket got my wallet, a mugger took my watch. All I have is a pen and a bunch of keys. Take them.' He threw them on the ground. Nobody even looked at them.

Maria frowned. 'You speak good Portuguese for a foreigner.'

'I need to for my job in England. We have a lot of links with South America.'

'You're staying in a hotel, then? How will you get there on one foot?'

She had to repeat it twice. The man was nearly at the end of what he could take, I could see it in the way he swallowed before replying: 'I'll hop there.'

Maria burst out laughing. She has a deep strong laugh – a boy's laugh that drags up the corners of your mouth despite yourself.

'You will hop? An Englishman hop through the streets of our city by night? Hop! Hop!'

And she started hopping with that manic energy of hers – she doesn't care what anyone thinks of her, just does what she wants to do, and in no time the kids were hopping round the man too, all laughing and squeaking in excitement. I like it when they remember they're still children. Even the man couldn't help letting out a chuckle – a chuckle cut short by a gasp of pain as Joca crashed into his ankle by mistake.

In a second, Maria was down by his side, squinting at the ankle.

'You cannot hop,' she said. 'And you cannot stay here on the street in the city in the night. It's death to foreigners.'

'I haven't got a choice,' muttered the man. Maria tugged his head round until he was looking her straight in the eyes. She stared into his face for a moment, stock still as she weighed him up. Then she nodded once with brisk decision and jumped away from him.

'You will come with us,' she declared. Luiz started to protest, but Maria turned and spat at his feet. His mouth shut up like a gate slamming. He reached into his belt for his knife, but Maria's knife was out faster. Luiz snarled something under his breath and melted into the shadows. I caught Maria's eye, but all she said was, 'Marco, Chico – lift him, gently, *gently*, I say! Now come on!'

The man was heavy between us as Chico and I pulled him up. I had never felt cloth like that of his suit, softer than the oldest jeans and smooth as honey. Still, he was as dirty as we were by now. I could feel him resisting, even as he staggered to his feet.

'Where are we going?' he said.

'Home!' called Maria over her shoulder. She was already away down the moonlight-splattered street. 'This way!'

Although we followed the gang as fast as we could, they could run like alley cats, and the man's awkward weight slowed me and Chico down. The man limped along between us, an arm slung over each of our shoulders, but the difference in our heights made it a lopsided stagger. The others disappeared like wisps of smoke, except Roberto, who is losing control of his legs. Luiz was nowhere to be seen.

Chico can never stay silent for long. What he lacks in height he makes up for in noise. He says he talks for the two of us.

'What you up to on our patch, then, Mister?' he chirruped.

I saw the blank look the man gave him.

'Chico says, "What are you doing here in the city?"' I explained.

The man's voice came through gritted teeth, but he spoke politely enough.

'I'm at a conference.'

'What?' Chico was intrigued.

'A place to learn, to discuss. It's about... management techniques.'

'Management? What's that then?'

'How to organise the people who work for you. I'm a manager – a boss – and I'm trying to get the best out of the people who work for me.'

'Lots of people working for you? You loaded, then?'

'Loaded? I don't...'

'Chico,' I suggested, 'cut the slang. Keep it simple, or he won't understand a word you're saying. He's learned his Portuguese from a book.'

'Loaded...' Chico thought a moment. 'Loads of dosh! Are you rich, Mister?'

'Richer than you, perhaps, Chico,' replied the man, as we stumbled along through the familiar tangle of streets in the warm darkness.

'Hey, Marco! The Mister, he reckons he's richer than us!'

I chuckled. 'Takes a lot to be richer than us, Chico,' I murmured.

We were going down a long stairway, and the man turned his face to me, puzzled. But before he could speak, he caught his foot on a step and hissed through his teeth in pain. In a flash, Maria turned, peering back at him, the whites of her eyes bright in the night.

'Can you go on?'

'Yes,' the man said.

He was brave.

'What are you going to do to me?' he muttered.

I smiled at him, trying to ease some of the fear, even if I could do nothing about the pain. 'You're safe with us. We're only street kids, but we will look after you. It's not far. Five more minutes. Come on.'

Chico chattered away on the other side of him but I could see the man was unable to understand either the street-language or the odd bits of normal Portuguese that Chico occasionally threw in.

'Quiet, Chico,' I said. 'Let him be.'

And at that moment, the man sagged between us:

the walk was too much for him, and with fear, pain and hunger, he had blacked out.

''Ria!' I called, struggling to hold up the dead weight. She was at my side in a second.

'Is he dead?' she asked.

'No!' I could feel his pulse strong and steady. 'But he can't go on.'

'We must get him to the car. You'll have to carry him, Marco, you're the strongest.'

Together we managed to lug the man over my shoulder so that I could hold on to his legs. I was glad it wasn't far.

We all helped to pass him and Roberto over the fence. Getting him into the back seat was tricky, and it was probably a good thing he was unconscious, as the older ones are clumsy and the little ones are rough. But we covered him with the blanket, and at a sign from Maria, I left the man so that I could settle Roberto, while Ze Pequeno and Junior crashed out in the front and Maria took the little ones below the shallow pit we had hollowed out under the car. They always said they felt safer there, out of sight. Chico grumbled at having to tell Zeze his goodnight story yet again, but in between my attempts at holding Roberto down on to his blanket I could hear the familiar story in which nothing happened '... *and he had a mum and a dad, yes and a leather football, a real leather one and they played lots together and they all lived happily ever after...*'

Roberto slipped away into either sleep or unconsciousness at last. Each night I wondered if he would ever wake up. As I slipped into my usual spot I heard Chico call something to Maria, and heard her groan, swear and heave herself up to get Junior changed. He still wets himself and it makes him cry great hiccupping ashamed tears. That night she didn't slap him, just talked to him urgently for a few minutes before she wriggled back down to the girls. There was a low mutter for a minute or so and I heard a whispered 'Amen'. Then it was quiet.

I had time to think before I fell asleep. What had Maria brought on us now? Who was this rich foreigner with his honey-smooth suit and his conferences? Why had he been in that part of town, a district where no foreigners go unless they're journalists or fools? And what were we going to do with him tomorrow? He needed to get back to his hotel, but how would he do it on a wounded ankle and no money? I thought of an ambulance coming to fetch him here, or the people in his conference driving up in their grand cars to collect him, and a great weariness came on me in the blue velvet of the night for I sensed that this man's arrival meant the end of our home. I sighed, because it was the best place we had found, and I must have sighed louder than I meant to, for Maria's savage whisper came up the side of the car:

'Eh, Marco! We're trying to sleep down here – cut the huffing and puffing.' She paused and added: 'Don't worry. All will be well, you'll see.'

I smiled in the darkness and settled down to listen to the younger ones muttering and screaming in their dreams. As ever, I knew I would spend most of the night awake, hoping in vain for sleep to shut out the life I led even for a few hours. But for now we were together: that was what mattered.

2

'Hey, the Mister's awake!'

Chico's shout brought me back from the junk pile. I looked through the glassless window of the car to see Chico nose to nose with the man. He looked bleary, as well he might. Chico waved his hand in front of the man's face.

'You awake, Mister?'

'Yes, I think so...'

'We had to carry you, Mister! You eat well at the conference I think! You're heavy!'

'I'm sorry you had to carry me.' He rubbed his eyes and blinked in the sunlight. 'Look, it's morning! What time is it? I must get back to my conference! Where am I?'

'You're in the car, Mister! Bet you've never slept in a car before, eh? We had to bunch up close to make room for you last night!'

The man looked around him. I saw our home through his rich eyes: a large decrepit shell of a car, its seats ripped out and its windows cracked. It had been crashed here by joyriders, anything valuable ripped out, and the rest left to rust away in the dust of the site.

The man was lying on a rough sack, Ze Pequeno's sweatshirt under his head as a makeshift pillow and a woven red blanket over him. It smelt slightly of sweat, strongly of the load of overripe bananas we brought back in it one day. He pulled it back and tried to sit up.

'No, don't try to get up.' The cool, commanding voice made him stop. It was Maria, sliding in through the front window. Chico sat back on his haunches.

'It's okay, the mister's better now, aren't you, Mister?'

'Yes, yes, much better. In fact, I'm fine now,' the man lied, as he began to get up. 'Look, I really must be getting back. My business... it's very important...' He stopped as a spasm of pain jolted through his ankle. In a flash, Maria was down beside him.

'You are not better. You are...' She stopped; her eyes narrowed, as if she didn't want to call attention to the man's feeble state, and then she grinned at him. 'You are hungry! And thirsty! I don't know what you're used to in the posh hotels of our city, but here we have our standards to maintain. We always invite our guests to breakfast before they leave on their *important* business. Chico! Marco! Take him outside so he can do what he needs to do. You'll need to use the back door – the VIP entrance! Bebe! Bring the senhor his breakfast in bed!'

Chico bounced up to his feet with a chuckle. 'Ohé, Marco – a hand here.'

Chico scrambled out of the front window, then helped me heave open the boot with a great screeching of rusty hinges so that we could haul the man out. He leant on our shoulders on the way to the sandpile. Then we went whistling round the corner for a moment or two before we helped him back towards the car and set him down in its shade. He was sweating with the effort of those few steps. I slammed the boot shut, making the shell shake. Chico laughed again.

'Breakfast now, Mister! It will be an honour!' He bowed low and shot off, shouting, 'Bebe! Bebe!' Maria settled down beside the man, her back comfortably against the rusty side of the car, and ripped a corner of cardboard off a box. 'Now we wait for room service!' She shoved the cardboard into her mouth and chewed it.

Before the man could reply, Chico was back, standing to attention at the window of the car. 'The Mister's Breakfast!' he announced, and bowed again. Bebe, who is a pretty little black-haired girl about seven years old, giggled, made a mock curtsey and presented him with a loaf of bread and a knife. She beamed at him, then made way for me to hand him the orange and the tin cup of water that I had saved him from my own meal. I leaned over a wing to watch him. The man couldn't help grinning back at us.

'Thank you, Madam, Sir. Your room service is excellent! Won't you share this feast with me? Or have you already eaten?' He started to cut the loaf of bread and passed a slice to the girl, Bebe.

'You eat it, Senhor,' she insisted. 'You are a big man. You need your food.' The man hesitated, then, as I nodded to encourage him, he fell on the food as if he hadn't eaten for days. Bebe curled up beside him and started stroking his sleeve, gazing up at him coyly until Maria called her off with a warning shake of her head. Bebe pouted, stuck her tongue out at Maria and stayed where she was. But she did stop pawing him. By the time he'd finished, the whole gang had left their jobs and gathered round the car, jumping up to peer in through the windows, or leaning on the frames to stare. The man who had looked at us with terror in his eyes the night before looked round at the circle of faces and grinned as if the joke was on him.

'Thank you,' he said as he finished up. 'Now I really do feel a lot better. I think we should become better acquainted.'

Caju hooted with laughter. 'The mister speaks posh!'

I prodded him in the ribs and hissed, 'Caju! He is our guest! We're only street kids and he is an important man – a foreigner. Show some respect.' I nodded to the man to carry on.

'My name's Peter Clark. And you are... Chico? Bebe? Marco?' We nodded, Chico obviously thrilled to be among the first known. The others introduced themselves from their stations around the car: Zeze and Gilvam holding their knives as if they would kill him if he set a foot wrong; Roberto, burbling some of his usual nonsense and laughing manically; Caju, half-hidden behind the wing of the car, ready to run; Ze Pequeno and Joca, trying to tell Peter Clark their entire life histories, oblivious to the fact that he understood about one word in thirty; Isabella, rocking backwards and forwards, a distant look on her face; Junior, arms clasped tightly round his chest, not knowing whether to shiver with excitement or terror...

Maria frowned. 'And you, Luiz?' she said.

I wondered when he had returned and where he had been. He pulled himself slowly off the boot of the car where he'd been slumped.

With a slight sneer, he said, 'Like you say. Luiz.'

Peter Clark turned to Maria. 'And you are...?'

She spat out the wad of paper she was chewing. 'Maria.'

Peter choked on his water. 'You mean, you're only a *girl*?'

Someone sniggered, then joined the rest of us in breathless silence.

Perhaps if things had been different, Maria would have been instantly recognisable as a girl. Perhaps she would have worn frilly dresses and had long hair and pretty jewellery. Maybe she would have giggled, and walked with tiny delicate steps, and played with dolls. But I don't think even a proper family with money and education would have managed to make Maria so different from what she is.

It's not that she isn't pretty. If you bother to look under the dirt we all struggle against, you notice her bones are very fine and the sweep of her jaw in particular is delicate. Her neck and throat have a soft vulnerability to them and her eyes, which are a peculiar blue-grey and heavily-lashed, are intelligent and miss nothing. She has the figure of a boy, that's true. But on the streets, girls often don't round into the soft curves that girls should grow into. Their bodies are muscular and thin and taut from watchfulness.

Maria's movements are those of a leader – decisive, strong, commanding. Yet she has a grace that shows in the way she wastes no energy in any movement, but follows through with precision just what she has to do. Her grace is that of her inner life – careful, tense, brave, laughing terror in the face.

But she keeps her hair cropped into tight short curls because of the lice, and wears the filthy jeans and T-shirts we all wear, boys and girls alike. And any of us would admit freely that it is unusual, to say the least, for a girl to be a gang leader here on the streets of the city. A girl usually needs the protection of an older boy or a man, however badly he then treats her. And it was dark last night: Peter's mistake was an easy one to make. Even so... *only* a girl?

Maria turned her head to look straight at him. '*Only* a girl?' she said softly.

Peter went very pale as if he remembered the circle of knives from the night before.

'Well...' he stuttered, 'I didn't mean... it's just such a surprise. I thought... well, the way the others, even the boys, do as you tell them. The way you seem to know what to do, even when you find idiots like me lying on street corners. I just assumed...'

'Have you no women leaders in your country, Mister Peter?' Maria asked in a voice that made Chico and the others shrink back a step.

'Of course we do!'

'And are you surprised when they know what to do in their jobs? When men obey them?'

'No, not at all. My boss is a woman—'

'Then *don't* be surprised at me!'

Peter took a deep breath. He looked straight at Maria for the first time. I saw admiration and a glimmer of laughter in his eyes.

'I'm sorry,' he said. He swallowed. 'To be honest, I would have been surprised at anyone, boy, girl, man or woman taking me in and looking after me last night. It was the action of a hero. I am... honoured to know you, Senhorinha Maria.' He bowed his head. There was a moment's silence.

Then Maria gave a shout of laughter.

'"Senhorinha Maria",' Maria spoke the words carefully, then gave another delighted shout of laughter. 'Sounds good, eh, Marco? Beats "Oy you! Gutter rat!" anyway!' She saw Peter looking confused and slowed her speech down again. 'Well…' Her manner became brisk as she jumped up and addressed the gang. 'Since you're all here, listen up. Bebe, you go with Junior and Caju to the market. See what you can pick up. Ze Pequeno and Zeze, over to the bus station to wash cars – the buckets are under the car. Gilvam, Joca, Roberto – you get down to the station and try to sell the last of the biscuits. Keep well away from the *cachaca* or there'll be trouble. Chico, Isabella and Luiz – you go to Sao Paulo. If you're quick, you'll beat the dustbin lorries.'

'Let them go to Sao Paulo. I'll do the mall,' said Luiz, who can never bring himself to do an honest day's work without complaining.

'No, Luiz. I know what you want to do there and I won't have it,' snapped back Maria.

'And just what is that?' asked Luiz, with a curl of his lip.

'You want to steal and pickpocket and trick people out of their money,' said Maria.

'Stupid people, who don't look after their money right. They deserve to lose it. Easier pickings than dredging through dustbins for scraps!'

Maria stood up. 'Luiz, while I lead this gang, we stay straight, do you understand? If it means we have to go hungry, we will stay out of the hands of the police.'

Roberto heard the word even in his doped state and let out a frightened yelp, hiding his head in his arms.

I crouched beside him and stroked him gently, feeling him flinch at every touch. 'No, Roberto, it's okay. The police aren't here. They won't hurt you again. We'll look after you.' It would be minutes before he would stop shaking. Maria rounded on Luiz.

'Now see what you've done! Go, before I get angry with you! All of you, go with God.'

'Go with God,' they chorused back and melted away in their small groups. Luiz slouched off, way behind Isabella.

'Chico!' called Maria in a low voice. The small boy turned. ''Ria?'

'Watch Luiz. Don't let him get into trouble.'

Chico nodded thoughtfully. 'He wants this gang, Maria. He wants to run it his way.'

'Never! We would all be dead within a month!'

'You watch him too, Maria. Go with God.' And Chico was gone.

Maria turned to me.

'Marco, stay with Mister Peter and keep him safe. I'm going to the clinic. If Doctor Gilberto can come today, I will bring him back with me. If not, it may mean an ambulance...'

We looked at each other and I knew her thoughts.

'The doctor will come for your sake, Maria,' I reassured her. 'Go with God.'

3

I would rather have gone on the streets and kept an eye on Luiz, but Maria is leader and too much time would be wasted if every one of her decisions was argued over. We have a council every week where we can make our opinions heard, but from day to day, we do what she says. Sometimes our lives depend on it.

I felt Peter watching me and turned my back on him for a moment. Alone with the rich English stranger, I felt shy and awkward. What would I say? How could a sewer rat like me and a manager from the other side of the world possibly find anything in common? Part of me was desperate to know him better – he had such laughing eyes; but most of me was running away to hide so that he wouldn't realise how inadequate and stupid I was. His voice broke the silence for me.

'Don't you need to go out to "work" too, Marco?'

I nodded, still with my back to him.

'Yes, but today I must wait with you until Doctor Gilberto comes.'

There was a pause. 'I'm sorry. I've interrupted your routine.'

I shrugged, more nervous than ever. Routine? What did my routine matter to someone like him?

'I shall work here and you shall rest. You would be

more comfy in the car.'

I collected the box of metal scraps and the wire wool, hesitated, then slid into the car beside him and squashed myself up in a corner as far away from him as possible.

'Wait, I'll shift over...' said Peter, moving up to make room for me. The tension in his body and the tightness round his mouth and eyes showed me he was still in pain, but I admired the way he said not a word about it. I would like that sort of courage. He watched me fumbling over the metal scraps, and again broke the silence. 'Tell me about yourselves. Who are you? Where are your homes? Why are you roaming the streets of the city late at night? Why aren't you at school? You're only ten or so, aren't you?'

I frowned and set to work to sort the scraps and polish them with scraps of wire wool. It wasn't that I minded being taken for a ten year old when I was nearly fourteen. Like I said, street kids' bodies are different. I suppose it's a question of diet. No, I was wondering how much to tell him, how much a rich man like him could understand of the way we live. We were worlds apart. I looked up to try to learn something of him from his looks.

He was a handsome man. Nearly thirty, I thought. Blond hair, cut short and would normally spring out healthily from his scalp, not be plastered down as it was from the rigours of the night. His eyes were pale blue, and looked at me without any scorn, just with concern and interest. There were lines round the corners, the sort that mean someone spends a lot of time smiling. The sort of suit he wore, the intelligence and good breeding he showed – people of his class were the ones who wrote letters to the newspapers to get us kids cleared off the streets. But looking into his face now, I couldn't imagine Peter Clark writing a letter like that. It was a strong face, a real man's face with tough pale skin over firmly-defined bone. If I had a father, I would like one with just such humour in his face, and just that gentle strength. Not a strength that knocked my mother halfway across the kitchen on to a hot stove... I felt the trembling begin, shut my mind and began to polish the metal scraps. He reached out and touched my hunched shoulder, like a father would perhaps. But how should I know? I turned away and he withdrew his hand.

'I'm sorry. I didn't mean to pry. It's just that I know as much about you as I do about aliens from another planet. And nothing you have said or done so far has been anything like what I would have expected from a *maloqueiro*, a street kid. *Who are you?'*

I stared at him. He really did want to know about us. So I told him. I chose my words carefully and explained the ones that puzzled him.

'There are many street children in the city. Their parents come from the country, thinking they will find work in the city, but there is none. The family grow poor; they have no food; they move into a cheap house where there isn't enough space for everyone. Sometimes they turn to drink – *cachaca*, maybe. Or glue, or drugs. They quarrel. The children run away from home and have nowhere to go. Or perhaps their parents die in a raid and the children are left with nothing.'

'A raid?'

'Every now and then rival gangs, especially the

older ones, have raids on their enemies. Many innocent people get in the way and are shot. Many are injured or killed. Maria's mother was killed in a raid. She heard the shooting, and ran out to bring her baby sister inside. They didn't come back. The house had been rented and the owner had new tenants for it. So José – her big brother – and Maria had nowhere to live. They came on to the streets and José found more kids who had no homes. He looked after them. He led the gang, until...'

'Until?'

'Until he disappeared. Last year. So Maria took over—'

'Just a minute,' said Peter, bewildered. 'Maria's brother disappeared? What do you mean? People don't just disappear!'

'In this country, they do. He went out to the dump one day on his own, looking for things to mend and sell. And he didn't come back. They searched and searched. But no one had seen him. They said the death squads had been in the area...'

'So you think he was arrested?'

'Maria swears he is still alive somewhere. But me? I think José was shot down like a dog in the street.'

Peter couldn't take it in. I went on.

'The death squads are groups of men, some police, some security guards, paid by the shopkeepers, who drive on to the streets with their guns, and...' I shrugged. 'You heard her say to the children, "Go with God"? You think that was just a thing to say, like "How do you do?" or "Goodbye?" Well, when we say that to each other, we mean it. We cannot protect the little ones all the time. We need extra help. Go with

God. But I don't know where God was when José disappeared.'

'Did you know him?'

I scrubbed at a stubborn spot of rust. How could I describe the times I had held Maria through fits of wild sobs as she mourned for her brother? As she told me stories of when they were young: the tricks they would get up to together, the adventures they had, the way he kept her hoping when the whole family had died and they were out on the streets with nothing but each other. The ingenious plans he put into action to keep them both alive, to keep her out of the hands of men who would abuse her. About the little ones who were attracted to him as if he was a Pied Piper: the way they would run to his arms for safety. His hopefulness for a future against all the odds, the trust in Jesus that never faltered for a moment, even in the darkest times; the honesty and integrity that coloured his whole life. So although I never knew him, his words and wisdom gave a shape and direction to my own life through his sister.

But Peter Clark was a stranger and such words are for sharing only with close friends.

'No, I never knew José,' I said. I looked up, very daring. 'And you, Senhor? What are you doing in this *favela*?'

Peter laughed a wry laugh. He didn't mind me asking! 'I was on my way back to the hotel after doing some sightseeing in parts of the city I hadn't visited before. A little lad, younger than you, picked my pocket. I chased him for what seemed like miles into the maze of streets without thinking about how I was going to get back. Then I tripped and bust my ankle.

Just when I thought things couldn't get any worse, some mugger cracked me on the head and made off with the little loose change I had left. Although any number of people went past – richer and better-educated than you, Marco – you were the only ones who stopped to help me. My thanks.'

I didn't think he owed the rest of us much. 'Luiz would have knifed you.'

'Maria told Luiz off when he wanted to go stealing?'

I frowned. 'It is wrong to steal. Maria will never hear of it. How can we ask God to be with us if we go out to steal? And besides, they might be caught and fall into the hands of the police. We will find enough to eat without stealing. But,' I smiled ruefully, 'it would be much easier to steal, I think!'

Suddenly I heard the sound of footsteps coming nearer. Footsteps that stopped just beyond the sand pile outside.

'Quiet!' I hissed and already the knife was in my hand.

'*Marco*!' whispered Peter. But I had crept out of the car and left him alone.

I could hear a man's voice. What if it was the foreman of the building site? It had lain abandoned so long now that we were tempted to think it could be our home for ever. The bulldozers and cranes seemed to sleep in between the dusty piles of earth and stacked up sacks of cement. It was only the fact that the site was so out of the way that had kept them all from being stolen ten times over. As far as I knew we were the only humans to go near the place in all the months we had been here. Was it all at an end?

4

I sidled silently around the sand pile to look, and one of the two figures swung round as if she had eyes in the back of her head.

'Ohé, Marco!' called Maria. 'The doctor is gracing us with his presence already.'

Doctor Gilberto gave her a mock cuff on the head but she ducked so that he was caught off-balance and staggered a little, laughing.

'Cheeky brat,' he grumbled. 'I have other business in this part of the city, and have just popped by with you because it happened to be convenient.' His voice dropped. 'Bring Roberto next time you come to the surgery. I'll see what I can do. And your headaches?' Maria flapped her arm and turned away as if to tell him not to bother with her. He grimaced and strode over to me. 'Marco, good to see you. How do you put up with this madcap?'

The doctor has always loved Maria, always found medicines she needed for the little ones without asking any questions, always dealt swiftly with the cuts and wounds on the children she has brought to him.

'Doctor Gilberto. It is good of you to come.'

'Perhaps I'll get some sense out of a fellow-male,' he said, ignoring Maria's snort of derision. 'Maria tells me you're harbouring a fugitive?'

I didn't understand him.

'You've rescued someone? An Englishman?'

'He's in the car.'

'Ah, at last, a man of few words, deep thoughts and much sense,' said the doctor, throwing his bag at me to carry while he took his jacket off, rolled up his sleeves and walked towards the car. 'Heave your front door open for me, Maria, and let's see what we've got inside.'

The door creaked again and Maria grinned at Peter's rigid face.

'Thought I'd abandoned you, Mister Peter?' she asked. 'Don't worry. I was bringing Doctor Gilberto up-to-date with all our news. I've told him all about you. He's come to see your foot.'

'Thank goodness for that!' said Peter. 'I was beginning to think I'd be stuck in here for ever.'

'But how ungracious! Doctor? This way!' Maria invited the doctor into the car as if she was a queen summoning an ambassador into her court. Peter wriggled to sit upright.

'Maria, your car's getting lower, or I'm getting taller,' came a grumble.

'You are getting old, Doctor, and you don't bend so easily!' said Maria. She is disrespectful to him. I don't know how he bears it, but I believe he likes it. He is in fact a young man, about the age of Peter. He wears jeans and no tie with his shirt, not like a proper doctor at all. He sat down at Peter's side with a grunt. Maria waved a hand in his direction.

'This is Doctor Gilberto, who I occasionally allow to help the little ones. Doctor, this is Mister Peter, our

Englishman.'

'Pleased to meet you, Mr...?' The doctor began manipulating Peter's ankle straight away.

'Peter Clark. Please call me Peter. Thank you so much for coming. It'll be good to be rescued. I must be getting back. Ouch...'

'To his important business,' said Maria gravely. Peter shot a suspicious look at her. He couldn't tell if she was teasing him or not.

'Maria, my plane for England leaves tomorrow. I have to be on it.'

'Hmmm,' said the doctor, tugging his foot around while Peter turned grey again. 'Well, that's possible. You've got a bad sprain, I think. It probably feels terrible at the moment. Rest it for a bit, then you'll be as right as rain. Could do with an X-ray, I suppose, but you probably have better ways of spending the rest of your stay in our city than sitting in hospital waiting rooms. I shouldn't bother. Nothing broken, as far as I can tell. Here we are.'

The doctor strapped up the ankle quickly and efficiently and gave Peter a foil wrap of pills to ease the pain. I hoped Luiz wouldn't see the pills.

The doctor sat back.

'Well, you're in a pretty pickle, I must say, Senhor Clark – Peter. What are you going to do?'

'Aren't you going to get me an ambulance?'

'I could.' The doctor glanced at Maria, who shrugged.

Peter didn't miss this. 'What's the problem?'

The doctor sighed. 'Peter, I could request an ambulance, but there aren't enough to cope with all the emergencies in the city as it is.'

'But I—'

The doctor continued as if he hadn't interrupted. 'Also, when they hear where you are, they might refuse to come and get you.'

'Why?'

'This building site is tucked away behind one of the most dangerous *favela* – shanty towns – of the city. An ambulance – or even a taxi – would conveniently get lost before they got as far as here and return without you.'

'But that's ridiculous! I've got insurance!'

'Also, even if they did make it here, it would mean...' Again the doctor glanced at Maria, 'it would mean that the officials would know where Maria's gang are housed, if this can be called housing.'

'So what's the problem?' Peter was annoyed at all these excuses. His chances of a nice comfy ambulance ride back to civilization seemed to be slipping away.

The doctor sighed and ran his fingers through his hair. I noticed how tired he looked. 'If the officials get to know, next the squads will find out. And then one night they will come in a black van with their machine guns while the gang is sleeping, and... just a handful more of disappeared ones. Just another inconvenience stamped out. And who will lift their voice to protest? Who will cry for them?

'So, Peter, if you want rescuing, I will fix it for you. But if you are willing to wait here while you recover, I know Maria and her gang will keep you as safe as they can. Perhaps Marco here could find a taxi that will pick you up from somewhere less... dangerous. Then you can make your own way back to your comfortable hotel and your important business. You must choose.'

I didn't look at Peter while he fought to come to a decision. The doctor had voiced all my fears. I prayed that he would make the right decision. Maybe he was even more desperate than before to get out of this crime-ridden *favela* where he could get machine-gunned down at any minute? Perhaps the officials already knew where we lived. Perhaps they were just waiting for tonight before they came out of the darkness to mow us down. Peter would be thinking of his conference, the important business he had to finish before he caught his plane back to England tomorrow. He was English, he was an adult, he was rich – he had no part in this.

'I'm afraid I must insist you find me an ambulance,' he began. I felt the cold thud of disappointment in my gut. But then he caught sight of Maria's face. 'What?' he snapped.

'Nothing. I'm thinking,' she replied.

'Why are you looking like that, then?'

I spoke over her impatient grunt. 'She's wondering how to tell the gang that they have to leave this place.'

And where *would* we go?

The doctor spoke softly. 'Have you the right to make them leave their only home, a home they have risked for your safety?'

Maria stopped him. She was angry. 'Mister Peter must look out for himself. He has important business. He is in pain. He has every right to an ambulance.'

Peter fought with himself for a moment. Then he said slowly, 'You're right, doctor. I'll stay here and rest, then I'll find my own way back to the hotel this evening after the siesta.'

The doctor looked relieved. Maria's face lit up.

'If we let you!' she teased, then held up her hand and was serious for a split-second. 'We will look after you.'

Peter grinned. 'I know.'

Doctor Gilberto packed his bag, but before he got up, he said, 'Maria, may I talk to Peter alone? No, Marco, you stay if you want. You talk less than a brick wall and understand more than most men twice your age.'

Maria shrugged and slipped out of the boot, leaving the three of us alone.

'I'm glad you made that decision,' said the doctor. 'Maria has enough to cope with already. Now, I think I can trust you, but still, I hate leaving her in this vulnerable position. Can you give me your assurance that you won't harm her?'

I looked up in surprise.

'How dare you suggest that!' said Peter angrily. Doctor Gilberto took him by the shoulders and shook him.

'Peter, I haven't the time or energy for your sensibilities. I need to get back to the clinic before they notice I've gone. Maria cannot be my responsibility – she's her own woman – but I care very much about her safety. Now, will she be safe with you? Do you promise?'

'I promise,' said Peter, taken aback by the intensity of the doctor's tone. 'But do you mean you should be somewhere else? Should I have come to your clinic?'

'The street children have to take their help where they can find it. How could they come to my clinic with some of the problems they have? They know I'll get out here if I can and I won't charge them or report them if they come to have gunshot wounds or stab marks treated, or if they get an infection from dirty needles.'

Peter looked baffled. 'Gilberto, you could stay safely out of all this – no one's dropped you into their lives like I've been dropped here. Why do you do it?'

The doctor smiled. 'You want the short answer or the long one?'

'The short one?'

The doctor looked at him steadily. 'To give back a little of the love that Jesus Christ has given me.'

Peter coughed in embarrassment and his gaze fell from the doctor's. 'And... er... the long one?'

'Because somebody has to! Because Maria's an amazingly brave, resourceful and competent girl and she's never had a chance! Because I can't bear the thought of her at the end of her resources and having no one to turn to! Because Jesus demands that we care for the voiceless ones first! Because she needs me! And if my coming to help her means that my wealthy patients have to spend a few minutes longer leafing through glossy magazines in my waiting room, so be it. You're a lucky man to have been found by Maria. She could teach you a lot.' He looked at me. 'They could all teach you a lot. Now I must go. Goodbye. Look after that ankle.' He nodded goodbye to me. 'Marco.'

'Doctor.'

And without looking back, the doctor left. Peter looked as if he'd stroked a kitten and found it was a tiger.

Maria was not long returning.

'So, Mister Peter! How do you feel?'

He recovered himself and grinned as if the joke was on him. 'Apart from seeing that faith in action is about as gentle as a... as a volcano, much better, thanks, Maria. In fact, now the ankle's bandaged up, it feels almost comfortable.'

It was a relief to me, too, to see the pain disappearing from his face.

'Good. The doctor is good to us. He works too hard, and cares too much. He takes his faith too seriously. He is a good friend. I have to go out. Will you rest here until the others come home? Marco will find anything you need.'

'Yes, of course,' replied Peter. 'Maria, wait, please.' She turned back. We both saw him blush. 'I haven't said thank you properly... for saving my life last night. If it hadn't been for you, I'd be dead meat.' He held out his hand.

She hesitated, then reached out and held it briefly. 'You are part of the family, Mister Peter. It is an honour to help you.' With a flashing grin, which turned the compliment into a joke, and a clout to my shoulder, she disappeared from sight.

5

'Is there anything else to eat, Marco?' Peter asked, peering round the car as if he expected to see picnic baskets appearing under the torn seats. 'I don't want to be a nuisance, but I didn't eat yesterday, and it's catching up on me.'

'And you are a big man. I expect you need more to keep you going than we do.'

I bent down to look under the car, and heard him slip down beside me to look. His ankle must be feeling better. The pain in his eyes had been replaced by an inquisitive concern.

'When did *you* last eat, Marco?' he asked.

I shrugged. Why should he be concerned with me? 'I eat when there is food.'

I was looking among the boxes, blankets and bags under the car. Peter stared at the reclaimed rubbish that was waiting to be sold on. There was also a battered guitar and a recorder of some sort, as well as the paper, rags and washed-out tin cans. I shoved the boxes to one side then caught my breath and swore.

'What is it?' asked Peter, startled at my anger. I started to hide what I had found, but shrugged. He was not the sort of man to throw up his hands in disgust, even at this shameful object.

I held out a filthy plastic bag. 'Glue. We can't get Roberto to break the habit. We thought he'd given it up, but it gets such a grip...' I stopped, not wanting to scare Peter. How could he, a rich Englishman, understand that sometimes real life was so impossible, you took any way out you could just to escape it for a few minutes? If you knew the glue or the lighter fuel or the *cachaca* rotted your brain in the end, well, how long could you expect to stay alive on the streets anyway? Roberto's family had treated him so badly he had a lot of memories to run away from.

I shoved the bag under the rubbish to show Maria later, and found what I was looking for. 'Here.' I held out a packet of biscuits. They were a little old, but if they hadn't been old, they wouldn't have been thrown away in the first place. Peter took some with a nod of thanks, grimaced slightly and began to eat. Experimentally, he let go of the car and limped a few steps away. He got on quite well.

It was peaceful on the building site. The only movement was the trickling stream of what we hoped was clean water that came from a broken pipe. The sun was gloriously hot.

Peter leaned against the huge pipes that hid our car from view and told me how much he loved this beautiful country with its warm climate, lively cities and breathtaking countryside. His brief brush with danger had almost made him determined never to set foot in the city again; now it was daylight he could envisage coming back regularly, as he had ever since he started this job.

I smiled and bent down over the scrap metal. I liked to listen, and he talked with a warmth and energy I hadn't yet heard from the frightened man we picked up last night. I liked to hear him talk of his love for my country. It was good to be just him and me like this.

But there was another noise behind his talking. I lifted a hand suddenly in warning and he fell silent, a puzzled look on his face.

Then he heard it too. Low voices coming towards the car. I thought at first it was the children returning. But when I listened carefully, I could hear that one voice was a man's. Doctor Gilberto again? Why would he come back? He hadn't said he would.

'Stay hidden,' I whispered. We inched forward until we could peer through the pipes and see who it was without being seen.

Two figures came into sight. I hissed between my teeth and Peter glanced at me, curious. It was Luiz. What was he doing back already? An older man in a black leather jacket, a heavy gold medallion and an earring slunk behind him. The man's face was pale, and his eyes were narrow slits. A foxy man, a sewer rat. I was glad Peter was out of the car; there was something conspiratorial about the pair as they slouched up to it.

Luiz called, 'Maria? You there? Englishman?' A pause. 'She must've taken him off to the clinic, or got rid of him somewhere. There's no one around. Now talk.'

The foxy man took out his wallet, peeled out a bank note and casually wafted it in front of his face. Luiz's eyes fixed on the note as if he was hypnotised.

'I need more *aviaozinhos*,' said the man. 'Reliable. Who know how to run if there's the slightest sign of being found out. Who are prepared to take risks. It will be...' he wafted the note again, '...worth their while. Easy money. And, of course, perks of the job.' He smiled, revealing crooked broken teeth.

'And you want my gang?' said Luiz.

'*Your* gang?' said the man, raising his sandy eyebrows. 'I was under the impression it was run by... a girl.'

'Yeah, well, anything can change, can't it?' said Luiz in his usual sullen tone. 'Once I tell the others how easy it is to get some money without grubbing around on rubbish tips or selling rubbish on street corners, they'll be putty in my hands.'

'Oh yeah? The word on the streets is that this... *girl* has a strong hold over them. That she nannies them. That she's straighter than a spirit level. That she even sees begging as a no-go zone, and makes them work to earn their living. What will this girl have to say for herself?'

'She will have nothing to say! She always gets back before the others in the evening. Who knows – she might meet with some nasty accident when she does. Then she'll be out of the way for good.'

'I get you. Yeah, we might as well lose her. She could prove to be an inconvenience. Can you see to it?'

'Leave it to me,' leered Luiz.

'I'll send one or two of the big boys down in case there's any unpleasantness, say, six o'clock? Leave the body to them. They'll know where to take it.'

Luiz nodded.

The man put his note away and flicked a coin at him. 'For your work so far. There'll be more when the girl has disappeared. Do not let me down, my Luiz. You wouldn't like what I do to people who let me down. Now show me back to the main street.'

We sat motionless, hardly breathing, as the scrape of their footsteps died away into the distance. I found my hand was on Peter's neck, holding him back in case he tried to move, and I released him quickly. Who did I think I was? Me – a smelly street brat, holding down an Englishman? A rich businessman? I felt myself go scarlet and rubbed the back of my neck in embarrassment.

But Peter didn't seem to notice.

'Did I really hear that?' he said in an undertone. 'Perhaps my Portuguese isn't good enough. What did that foxy man want the gang to do? Be '*aviaozinhos*'? What have aeroplanes got to do with the gang?'

'Little aeroplanes – it's a street term. It means the children who deliver drugs. Many street kids earn their living this way.'

'But not you.'

'Not us. Not in a million years. It's dangerous. You hang out with the filth of the streets and... it's wrong. José would never have heard of it. Maria would not hear of it. We have all seen what drugs have done to our families.'

I replied to him with only half my mind on what I was saying. I was desperately trying to think what was to be done. Maria would come back in the early evening, and at six o'clock, Luiz and two of Fox-Face's assassins would be waiting to kill her. Even with Peter and me here, how could we stop them? What sort of a fight could an injured man and a boy put up against the sort of men these would be? There would be three bodies to take away, not just one. And who would look after the gang then? My thoughts whirled in that panic of indecision that happens when you have time to reflect, but not enough. Then there were footsteps behind us.

'Boo!'

Peter and I jumped round in terror. I had hold of the newcomer's hair and my knife was an inch from his throat before I realised who it was.

'*Chico*! Don't ever do that again!'

He shook himself free and chuckled. 'Eh, Marco, you're getting slow and lazy! I could have knifed you where you sat. And Mister Peter – you must learn to listen and not sit with your back left open to any stray knives that might hang around the neighbourhood. Have a banana. How is your foot?'

'Shut up, Chico. Maria's in danger.'

Instantly the small boy was serious.

'Danger? What do you mean?'

I explained what we had overheard. From Peter's expression, I saw that the conversation had been too much in slang for him to understand more than the odd word. They should teach real Portuguese in business schools. The news of the danger to Maria came as much of a shock to him as it did to Chico. Chico pursed his lips and whistled.

'So we were right,' he said.

Peter looked puzzled. I explained: 'This is something we've been concerned about for some time. There was word on the street that Luiz had been seen in the company of The Fox. Obviously they've got beyond just passing the time of day.'

'The Fox?'

'Fox-face,' said Chico, spitting in disgust. 'He's not even a drug baron, only a middleman who won't get his hands dirty. He pays street kids like us to deliver his rubbish to his customers and bring back the money. If the kids get caught, The Fox is nowhere to be found and the kids are left to take all the blame. Drugs!' Chico spat again.

'Chico's mother died an addict to heroin,' I said softly.

'It wasn't her fault!' flashed back Chico.

'I know,' I replied. 'She was tricked into it by the likes of The Fox. But it left you penniless.'

'And motherless,' said Chico. 'If I ever get my chance to be revenged on The Fox or one of his gang, they'll regret what they did to my mother.' He took two savage paces away then slammed his fists against the concrete pipe, spitting out a gush of vicious swear words as if they were vomit. He hides his memories well but sometimes they bubble up to the surface and the pain comes out in words. He threw himself against the pipe, panting, then craned his neck up as if he was in pain, eyes screwed up against the sun. His words came out between clenched teeth. 'So, Marco! This could be my chance! Let's warn Maria first, then get the gang together and smash Luiz's face in the dirt.'

'We know where she'll be at this time of day,' I nodded. 'No time to lose. You stay with Peter.'

'No, I'm coming with you!' Chico snorted. 'If anything happened to you and Maria came back on her own—'

I turned to the man who was still reeling from the situation he found himself in. Not just hauled off to a car by a bunch of drug-abusing, knife-wielding street kids, but now in the middle of a possible – I didn't dare even think probable – murder case. I crouched down beside him. 'Will you be okay by yourself? I wouldn't leave you, but this is urgent.'

'No, wait,' he stammered. 'The main thing is to get you all out of here to a place of safety. You can warn Maria and get her and the little ones to... oh, I don't know, an orphanage, or something? You'd be safe there, all of you...' He stopped, seeing our faces set.

I shook my head. 'The state children's asylums? You must be mad!'

Chico took Peter's arm and pulled him down so that they were face to face. Chico was very pale. 'They kill children there. They rough them up, or sell them to kidnappers. They're terrible places. Why do you think we preferred the streets?'

'Joca was sent to one when he had nowhere else to go – you should have seen his bruises when he escaped,' I added, remembering the hunched-up ball of terror Maria had found in the sewer. 'He still has nightmares about it.'

'Forget I mentioned it,' said Peter hurriedly, taken aback by the ferocity of our reaction. I got up.

'Yeah, well, see you later, Mister Peter,' I called out over my shoulder.

'I'm coming with you,' said Peter.

Chico and I stopped dead.

'But you can't walk! Your ankle!'

'It's much better now the doctor has been. I was going to make my way back to the city centre this evening in any case. I've got plenty of time to help you sort out this mess before I go.' He hesitated, then added, 'I won't hold you up. *Please* let me come with you.' I wondered if he had ever said please to a child before.

'Well, Mister Peter!' said Chico with a grin, 'if you're set on coming, how can we stop you? We would be honoured to be graced with your presence!'

'Cheeky toad,' growled Peter. 'I'll hobble as fast as you can walk.'

'If you're sure,' I said, 'then let's go. It's not too far.'

'Let me just hide these under here for the little ones when they return,' said Chico. He dived into his sack and brought out a bag of bread buns, some barely-touched pizzas and a box of peaches, which he stowed under the car. 'Ah, what these rich people throw away!' he sighed. 'Only a little stale, only a little bruised and plop, into the dustbin they go. All the more for us.'

'I'll think twice before I fill up my dustbin at home,' said Peter with a rueful lift of his eyebrows. 'If I ever get home...'

'You don't need to come,' I assured him. 'Rest here like the doctor said, then leave this afternoon before the gang get back. You could be safely back in your hotel by evening.'

Peter shook his head. 'If your opinion of my courage is that low, I'd better do something to repair it. Anyway,' he grinned, 'I wouldn't miss this adventure for anything! All for one and one for all. Off you go, D'Artagnan!'

Chico and I shrugged at each other, but Peter just laughed and pushed us on our way.

6

We set out across the building site, scrambled through the hole in the wire fence, and walked off into the *favela*, the slum town. Wooden huts stood alongside winding mud paths, with open sewers running either side. Often these sewers were blocked with food cartons, tins and revolting stinking masses of waste. Piles of rotting rubbish lined the paths. Pigs grunted from between the shacks. An evil-looking sheep crammed itself into a small patch of shade. The stench was high in the warm sun. We made our way unhesitatingly through the labyrinth of paths. Peter limped along a few paces behind us, only occasionally catching his breath when he stumbled on some rubbish on the path. We were given a few curious stares as people took note of our strange group – one small cheeky-faced youngster, one lean wiry boy and an unshaven and tousled pale-faced man with a limp following behind. Several people we knew called out greetings and we shouted back.

We turned into an alley where the housing went up a notch or two. This was no longer a shanty town, just a down-at-heel area with proper streets and small squares. Two women carrying briefcases almost bumped into us as we rounded a corner. The taller one backed off at a run, dragging her friend with her: 'Look out! It's some of those disgusting lice!'

'They should sweep them off the streets,' agreed her friend. 'They're vermin. Parasites. Mug you as soon as look at you.'

'Filthy little beasts.'

Peter had stopped in his tracks, staring at the women.

'*What* did they say?' he asked.

I saw the taller woman notice him and reach into her bag – was she just getting out an alarm or was it a gun? I didn't want to stay and find out.

'It's nothing. It's what everyone round here thinks of the street kids. It's what we are. Parasites. Come *on*!' Peter was opening his mouth but I ran after Chico so that he was forced to follow. We ducked between narrow houses with washing strung across between windows just above our heads.

'Short cut,' said Chico and strode on for another few minutes, past a road cleaner that was supposed to be hosing down the streets, but whose driver was taking a liberal approach to siesta hours. We carried on past a bar, a corner shop and more houses.

Suddenly Chico stopped dead with me and Peter hard on his heels. We all heard it; a scuffle ahead of us, grunting, panting, thudding, crunching – the unmistakable noises of a fight.

'Turn back! Let's go the long way round,' muttered Peter.

'See who it is first,' I said. Chico had already loped ahead, tucked well into the shadow of the buildings, and peered round the corner. He rushed back.

'Three to one! And the one's going down fast!'

'What are we waiting for?' I said, but Peter held on to my sweatshirt, making the hole in the back bigger.

'You're not going to get involved in a scrap, are you? You don't know who it is! We've got to get Maria! We can't waste time here!'

'Mister Peter! Ease up! This will be fun!' chuckled Chico.

'Peter! Maria would never forgive us if we passed by on the other side. Let me go!' I whipped away smartly and followed Chico round the corner. Peter groaned and, seeing no choice, followed on reluctantly.

The fight that met our eyes was totally one-sided. Three men were laying into a lad who had curled up on the floor in a defensive ball. The three were kicking and thumping with venom, laughing as each blow went home. Chico and I flew in and began a well-practised attack from the rear. We can't read and we've never written a word in our lives, but what we can do is fight! We are used to working as a team and seem to be able to read each other's minds. Within a few seconds we had winded two of the thugs. The other left the lad on the ground and turned to face the two of us with a snarl of anger. His hand went to his pocket and came out holding something glinting: a steel blade curved as cruelly as a cat's claw. I heard Chico's laugh and Peter's groan. As the thug swiped at us, we dodged and wove, trying to break the man's defences, while he was backing towards Peter.

I was wondering how long we could play him, when to my surprise Peter stepped quietly forward, tapped the man on his right shoulder so that he whirled round to the right, while Peter dodged to the left, grabbed him by the shoulders and swiftly kneed him in the groin. The man went down with a gasp of anguish, clutching himself and dropping his knife, which disappeared into Chico's pocket. Peter was gripping his ankle and muttering something in English which I didn't understand, but could guess at.

'Nice work, Peter!' I gasped. 'Didn't know you had it in you.'

'Nor did I,' he chuckled through gritted teeth. 'You're having a terrible effect on my morals, Marco!'

'Now we get out of here.'

Working as a three this time, we grabbed the young lad who was lifting his head groggily, and bore him off before the three thugs could lift a finger. We raced round a corner, down the street and out of sight. We didn't stop until we found an empty shed where we turfed out an indignant goat and sat in a rumpled heap, fighting for breath.

The boy spoke first, wiping the trickle of blood off his chin with the back of his fist.

'Thank you. I think you saved my life. I was coming down the road and they just picked on me.'

'Why?' asked Chico. 'Did you have money?'

'Nothing worth stealing,' said the boy, holding out a handful of small notes and coins. 'I looked different from them and they wanted someone to fight. I just happened to be in the wrong place at the wrong time.' He investigated his injuries impersonally. 'Nothing to cry about. And you? Are you hurt? Senhor?' He was obviously anxious.

'No, no,' said Peter, swallowing another couple of painkillers. 'I'm fine.' He looked at the boy in front of him, trying to size him up. The boy was perhaps a year or two older than me. He had sad blue-grey eyes, an unusual colour in this country; a fine-boned face and, despite his beating, moved with athletic grace. He was dressed in a shabby, grubby shirt and jeans. His face was old as if he had seen too much pain, and his mouth was set in rigid lines of determination. But there was also a warmth about him that made him approachable. Peter held out his hand. 'Peter Clark,' he said. The boy shook his hand, his grey eyes scanning Peter's face with a grave curiosity.

'Rodrigo.'

Chico and I also exchanged names with him. But Chico was impatient to know more about the fight.

'Look, are you saying those louts just jumped you for no reason?'

'Seems so,' said Rodrigo. Peter, Chico and I looked at each other. Peter looked younger, almost a boy.

'They can't get away with that,' he said. 'Look, we've got till evening before we need worry too much about Maria. Couldn't we make sure they think twice before they pick on innocent pedestrians again?'

'Oh, Mister Peter!' breathed Chico.

'Do you have something in mind?' I asked.

'You should smile more often, Marco – it suits you,' said Peter, to my surprise. He had looked at me enough to know me a little! I know I am often called serious, but I like to laugh too. It's just that there isn't usually much to laugh about. Rodrigo's stern features relaxed into a beam of pure mischief.

Peter grinned. 'I seem to remember running past a street-hosing tanker a little way back. What would you say to... borrowing it for a minute or two?'

And so it was that a few minutes later I stood panting on the corner to watch a shy-looking Englishman tap on the window of the tanker and wave at the driver who reluctantly put down his newspaper and wound down the window.

'Yeah?'

'I'm terribly sorry to disturb you, but I have absolutely no idea where I am,' said Peter with perfect truth and in tourist Portuguese. 'Would you mind telling me how I can get to the city centre?'

The driver sighed. Another foreigner! All these tourists getting lost. You simply had to take pity on them.

'I need to go to the bar in any case,' he grunted. 'I'll take you as far as there, then you can easily find your way on your own.'

'So kind of you,' murmured Peter, giving a thumbs-up sign behind his back. The driver heaved his fat body out of the cab and beckoned to Peter to follow him down the road. He waddled some way down the street, round the corner and, standing outside the small bar, gave Peter loud, slow instructions of how to reach the city centre. Peter thanked him in terrible Portuguese.

'You must have a drink on me,' he said, thrusting some of Rodrigo's coins into his hand. He watched through the window as the driver settled down at the bar with a bottle of red wine and a look of placid contentment. Then he hurried back to the tanker.

I slipped down the pavement.

'He's left the keys!' squealed Chico. 'You don't need to hot-wire it, Mister Peter. And Rodrigo's on the hose! And Marco is back! Here's a hat for you – disguise, eh?'

'The thugs are still in the square!' I panted.

'Then let's go!' said Peter, pulling on the hat and swinging himself up beside Chico in the cab. 'No, you drive, Chico. Why should I have all the fun?'

I jumped on to the back with Rodrigo, and Chico turned the ignition, setting the tanker trundling slowly down the road. We rounded the corner which led into the square. Chico slowed down. Rodrigo and I peered around the edges of the tanker.

'They've seen the road cleaner,' Rodrigo whispered. 'They're taking no notice. They're comparing injuries, I think. They haven't seen us on the back yet... Left a bit, Chico, give room for manoeuvre... ready, Marco? *Now*!'

As Peter flicked the switch that sent water flooding through the hose at enough force to blast unsightly rubbish off the street, Rodrigo and I heaved up the nozzles and turned them onto the three louts, so that in a split second, all three were knocked to the ground by the force of the water, and drenched from head to foot in the icy blast. They were so taken aback that they made no effort to get up, but sat dripping in the mud, gaping at the retreating tanker like three shocked toads. Rodrigo and I cheered.

'*Yo*!' shouted Peter from the cab. 'Back to base, Chico!' Chico put his foot down and the tanker bowled crockily out of sight back to its parking space.

We were just in time to bail out and watch a tipsy driver stagger to the cab of the tanker, cover his head with his newspaper and fall asleep.

It was an hour later. Rodrigo had insisted on spending his remaining money on food and drink, and I had brought the three of them to my favourite spot.

'We must celebrate in style,' I told them, 'and this is the perfect place.'

I made them wait behind a wall, then darted back to them, beckoning.

'We're in luck!' I whispered, as I led them through a gate in the high security fencing. 'The guards must be taking a break. Come this way, quickly.'

I had brought them to the park in the city centre. It was green and fresh. There were thick shady trees, brightly coloured tropical flowers and a small lake with a bamboo bridge over it. Birds sang. It was clean, tidy and there was no one about.

They followed me up to a clump of trees planted on a hilltop and we threw ourselves down in the dark cool shade. The view over the city was magnificent. It shimmered in the heat, all white and red around us.

'My city,' I said.

'And mine!' said Chico. 'But right now, let's eat! What did you get us, Rodrigo?'

With a grin, Rodrigo pulled from his bag a feast of a huge loaf of fresh crusty bread, yellow cheese pristine in its paper wrapper, a bag of fat juicy nectarines and a bottle of wine. The four of us threw ourselves on the food and devoured it in silent relish. There is something very beautiful about fresh food.

'It's as if my senses have suddenly come to life,' said Peter, juice dripping down his chin. 'Everything tastes more vivid than ever before.' He grinned at me almost as if he was giving me the credit for the way he was feeling. I could feel myself grinning back, relaxing into this strange feeling of being approved of by an adult, even liked…

'To the fat driver of the Hosing Van!' called Chico, raising the bottle and drinking.

'To the fat driver!' we answered, and fell about laughing.

I felt suddenly joyful to be alive, to have a full belly and friends to laugh with.

'And where do you live, Rodrigo?' asked Peter, when the last crumbs had been picked up with wetted fingers from the bottom of the bag.

'I come from a farm out in the country, an hour from the city. At least, that's where I think I come from.'

'What do you mean?'

'It's the only home I've known, but I only remember being there for a little while. I remember waking up in the stable there, but I can't remember anything about my life before that. The farmer gave me the name Rodrigo. He thought I must have been hit on the head and that I would never get my memory back. I had nowhere to go, so I stayed with him and worked for him.'

'Weird,' said Chico, sucking a nectarine kernel.

'He was a hard man, a cruel man in many ways, but the farm was so beautiful – there was a clean river, and a place where it got deeper so you could swim and dive. There were trees even bigger than these' – he motioned with his hands – 'all around it. You could work in the fields all day and keep out of his way. I suppose I was happy there.'

'So why did you end up in the city?' Peter asked.

'The local priest saw how the farmer treated his servants – his slaves we were, really. He talked to the farmer, advising him to change his ways. The farmer refused to treat us better and threw the priest out. Soon afterwards, the police came and arrested the farmer. We heard he went to prison. The farm was put up for sale. The priest offered us a home with his family, but I thought I would come to the city and see if I could find anyone who could tell me who I was. To see if I have a name. To see if I have a family of my own.'

And the longing in Rodrigo's eyes made me swallow and look away quickly. He at least still had a hope, however small, of finding someone to care for him and him alone. Of his father's arm across his shoulders, ruffling his hair. I knew my father was dead. And worse than that knowledge was my guilt that I was glad he was dead.

'I... hope you find them,' said Peter.

'Do you have a family, Senhor?' asked Rodrigo.

'No, I don't have much of one, really. I've lived away from my parents for... what... eight years now. And I'm not married.'

'Yet!' shouted Chico. 'A fine important rich man like you should have no trouble finding a wife!'

'She'd have to be a pretty amazing girl,' laughed back Peter. 'The right one just hasn't come along yet.'

'Hey! You! What do you think you're doing?' came a raucous shout from below.

'Oh no! I thought we were lucky! The guards!' I said, the sweat starting up under my arms. I shoved all the rubbish into the bag. 'Run!' The three of us sped off down the hill away from the two guards running up towards us.

'But this is a public park!' shouted Peter to our backs. 'Anyone can come in here!'

I groaned as I ran. Did he really not know anything about our city?

We stopped dead.

A third guard had appeared in front of us. He casually produced a revolver. We stared at the barrel, not moving a muscle. There was a click. But before we had time to decide whether to risk running or stay and be arrested, Peter stumbled down and put himself between us and the gun. He was either stupid or brave.

'*What is going on?*' he said, more angry than I had yet heard him. 'Put that gun away before someone gets hurt!'

The guards turned on him in surprise, matching up his foreign accent and his shabby clothes with his obvious air of authority. Peter took advantage of their bewilderment.

'What do you mean by shouting at us and scaring us out of our wits?' he demanded. 'This is a public park and we have every right to be here.'

'Street kids have no rights... Senhor,' growled one of the guards, not yet sure of Peter's status. 'And they are expressly forbidden from using the parks.'

'That's ridiculous! Where are we supposed to go? The streets are riddled with danger!'

'And it's our job to keep the park safe, Senhor, so that honest law-abiding people can come here and not be in fear of their purses and their lives. And that means no street kids. Right? Now, this once, you can all go. I won't take you in. But if I catch you here again—'

Peter started to protest again. But Chico and I grabbed his arms and propelled him to the gate.

'No, Peter. Let's just go while the going's good,'

I murmured. 'We have to warn Maria, not get ourselves thrown in jail, remember?' Reluctantly, Peter allowed himself to be pulled out of the park and back into the baking heat of the city. We tugged him along the dusty pavement any which way to get out of sight of the three guards who were still poised at the fence, hands on revolvers. I didn't dare meet Chico's eye.

'That is absolutely despicable!' fumed Peter. 'I can't believe he just said that! "Street kids have no rights"! We're human beings, aren't we? Just like him and his kids? Where does he expect us to have a picnic? And why come up against just four of us armed to the teeth?' He rounded on Chico and Rodrigo and me. 'And what are you all laughing at?'

In fact, now we were out of sight of the guards, Chico and I were folded double, clutching our stomachs in helpless fits of laughter, while even Rodrigo was grinning widely.

Peter was furious. 'What's the joke?'

I recovered enough to wag my finger at Peter, while Chico whacked him on the back.

'Mister Peter, you said "we"! That guard was ready to shoot us for being street kids and you said you were one of us! *You*! The rich English boss from half a world away with all your important business and hotels and nice suits – a street kid!'

And Chico collapsed into laughter again.

'I didn't mean I was one of you, I...' And Peter hesitated. He obviously hadn't noticed how he'd instinctively identified himself with us. Was he so different from us after all? He shrugged. 'Those guards just annoyed me. I don't like people who reckon they're more important than other people. And I was enjoying my picnic!' He turned to Rodrigo. 'Thank you for spending your last few coins on us.'

Rodrigo shook his head. 'It was the smallest thing. I owe you my life. Now I'm sorry but I have to leave you. You have to find your Maria, and I must carry on searching for my family. We may meet again. I hope... very much... that we will. If I can ever help you – with something more than a picnic – I swear I will. Go with God, my friends. I won't forget you.' He shook Peter's hand, squeezed my shoulder and thumped Chico on the back.

We watched him lope down the street and give one final wave as he disappeared round the corner. We waved back and I saw a curious expression on Peter's face.

'We'll bump into Rodrigo again, Peter,' I said. 'The city is large, but on the streets you meet up again and again.'

'Yes, you probably will,' replied Peter, 'but my plane leaves for England tomorrow – I won't see him again. And he spent his last money on me.'

7

'So how far away will Maria be?' demanded Peter, as he tottered after me and Chico. 'Are you two made of steel? Don't you ever need a rest? We must have crossed half the city by now.'

I leaned against a broken-down wall halfway up a steep road and waited for him to catch up. There was sweat running down his forehead and his mouth was twisted shut against the pain.

'Not far now,' I said.

'That's what you said half an hour ago,' muttered Peter, treading in a pile of something unmentionable before I could point it out to him. He groaned. I shrugged.

'No, really, we just have to get to the top of this hill and she should be there.'

'Shall we carry you again, Mister Peter?' chirped Chico.

'Get lost,' threw back Peter. 'I've got this far – I'll manage the rest.' He gritted his teeth and hobbled on.

At the top of the hill, we threw ourselves down panting in the shade of a white building. Peter shakily popped another painkiller out of its foil and swallowed it.

'Now we wait,' I said. 'She won't be long.'

'What is this place?' asked Peter.

But before I could answer, a door was flung open, and a chattering stream of children erupted into the street. A small group of them caught sight of Chico and me and bore down on us, full of the latest gossip from the streets.

Someone produced a battered football. There was the usual fight as to who would go on which side. I managed to make sure they didn't all come with me, and soon had them evenly matched. In no time there was a passionate game going on, with Chico zipping in and out of the opposing team's defences like a bee, and me out on a wing.

I left the game for a second to try to heave Peter up on to his feet.

'Come on, Peter – our side is one player short. Even a hopping one is better than none!'

Peter groaned. 'Marco, I can't! Give me a break—' The ball came straight towards him, but before he could choose either to fight me off or join the game, a slim figure slipped up behind him, whipped the ball from beside him and shot a straight hard kick right into the goal. He turned in surprise.

'Maria!'

'Too slow, Mister Peter!' she grinned. 'I didn't expect to see you all the way up here. Your ankle is better, then?'

'Much better, thanks – though I can't say I'm up to playing football.'

'Why didn't you go back to your hotel if you can walk?'

I suddenly remembered that our business with Maria was even more pressing than the game of football.

'Something important's come up. Peter insisted on coming to tell you. Is there somewhere we can talk?'

'Important business?' murmured Maria, looking at Peter through narrow eyes.

'Stop teasing the man,' I said.

'Pah,' she snorted and turned. 'Come this way.'

I tackled, shot the ball down the wing and left with a wave to the roar of protest.

'You still have Chico!'

Peter and I followed Maria back towards the white building. She stood to one side to let him go in. It turned out to be little more than a large covered barn with rough wooden benches in rows at one end facing a tatty chalkboard on a makeshift easel and a packing case cupboard. There was a door at the far end. A young woman with thick black hair falling down to her waist was cleaning down the chalkboard. She stopped with a jolt when she heard Peter, and thrust a hand into the desk in front of her without taking her frightened eyes off him.

'It's OK, Tania,' said Maria, coming round in front of Peter. 'He's with us.'

'Don't do that to me, Maria,' said the woman, rubbing her forehead with the back of one hand. 'Good afternoon, Senhor. I'm sorry to be so unwelcoming—' Peter took a step back when he noticed that her other hand was holding a revolver '—but we have had one or two less friendly visitors in the past. Marco, you should have known better.' But she matched her words to a hard hug and kiss of greeting.

Peter held out his hand to her. 'I'm Peter Clark,' he said. 'I'm sorry I startled you.'

'This is Tania Miguele,' said Maria. 'She's our teacher.'

Tania put her revolver away and took Peter's hand.

Peter did a double-take. 'Your teacher? You mean, this—' he waved his free hand round the bare room '—is a school?'

'I know it's not much to look at,' said Tania, 'but at least it's got a roof, so we can work here in the rain or in the heat of the day if we have to.'

Peter peered around. 'But where do you keep the books? The paints and things?'

'We don't have many books. I keep them at home so that they're safe. We have a little paper and some pencils that a shopkeeper gave us. If we had any more equipment, it would only be stolen,' Tania shrugged.

'How can you teach without books, without stationery? Doesn't the government give you money for that sort of thing?' he asked.

'It does pay for schools, of course,' said Tania, as she turned back to the chalkboard. 'But with this being a special school, it's harder to get money out of them. The forms take so long to fill in; the officials still aren't convinced Anna and I aren't trying to embezzle money from them; everyone is so obstructive. And in the meantime, the children need to be taught.'

'What do you mean, this is a special school?' puzzled Peter.

'Tania and Anna – she's gone home now – they teach the street kids!' said Maria, a warm smile lighting up her face. 'We can't get to normal schools – most of the street kids can't commit themselves to regular times to turn up to school – not many alarm clocks in the *favelas*! So Tania started this school for

us. We turn up whenever we can – and she teaches us.'
She slid over to a cupboard.

Peter stared at Tania. I wondered what he was
seeing. I guessed the sight of Tania was a welcome one
after seeing only us for a whole day. Tania's better
than us. She comes from a home where she was able to
stay and be brought up properly by two parents. Two
parents! And they have money too. She told me once
about her family's house with its swimming pool and
maids and meals that go on all evening. She dresses in
clear bright colours – that day she had on a blue dress
that looked like a wave of the sea. She is clean – I think
she has a shower every day – and smells not of sweet
and sour sweat, or urine, but like warm ripe fruit. Her
teeth aren't yellow and crooked but white and
gleaming. Her breath is sweet and fresh, not thick with
gum disease like ours. And her hair isn't lank and lice-
ridden, or speckled with white flecks from scalp
problems, but it is like the night itself, thick and black
and mysterious. And she is clever – I think she went to
college.

'What are you doing here, Tania?' asked Peter. His
arm sketched out the bare walls, the emptiness. We
could hear the foul language shouted out in the yard
from the children playing. I agreed with Peter. It was a
dump. We belonged in it: Tania didn't. But at Peter's
words she threw down the duster and marched up to
confront him. The top of her head came up to his
shoulder.

'You sound like my parents!' she snapped. Maria
whirled round to see what had made her so angry.
'"Why are you wasting your time with those *rats*?"
they say to me. "They're hardly human! You're worth

more than that! You're letting yourself down! Have you heard what our friends at work, at the club are saying about you? They laugh at you! They think you're just getting it out of your system before you find a real job, or better still, a husband".'

Peter's mouth hung open as she carried on: 'Well, I happen to believe that following Jesus means more than going to church on Sundays!'

'You too?' muttered Peter, but she stormed over him.

'When he said, "Love the people round you like you love yourself", he meant it. He didn't care whether people were rich or poor, whether they were important adults or kids off the street – he did what he could to look after all of them. Anna and I are his hands and feet here in the *favelas*. And we can't give these children much, but what we can give them is an education. And if that means I don't get a nice job in a nice school with nice children from nice homes, well, that's fine by me!'

'Or a nice husband,' I reminded her. She told me to shut up.

Peter had backed off from her vehemence, but he was grinning. I nodded.

'Another volcano,' I agreed.

Peter saw Tania's frown and quickly changed the subject. 'You must get some interesting students!' he said, looking at Maria. I could see he was imagining trying to teach her – imagining her stubbornness, her independence, her cool distance in a classroom.

'Oh, I do. I'm spoilt,' she replied, following his gaze.

Maria had fished a dogeared copy of a child's book

out of the cupboard and was poring over it, her lips moving silently.

'Look at her,' went on Tania. 'That girl started coming here only a little while ago. She couldn't read, couldn't write. She can only come one or two afternoons a week as she has work elsewhere to do. But she's so keen to learn that she's able to read simple stories now. She can write, after a fashion. She's got the hang of the basic maths I've had time to teach her. She's fallen in love with the poetry I've read to her. She listens to the little music I've got on tape as if she hears angels singing, she asks endless questions about her country, its history and the way it's governed – teaching Maria, it's like lighting a candle, it's like giving bread to a starving person, it's like turning water into wine.'

I watched Peter rearrange his thoughts as he took on board Tania's intensity.

'If only she had a chance in life,' Tania went on. 'She works like a dog. She fights for the souls of her gang and yet what future can there be for her? Even with my help, she's still condemned to the gutter. If I didn't trust that somehow she's being looked after, I would despair.'

'Looked after?'

Tania frowned again. 'You haven't seen her faith?' When Peter looked wary, Tania went on. 'Her mother went to my church. She passed her beliefs on to her children. Maria always needed to understand more about what it means to trust God than most adults do. So did her brother, José, before...' Tania turned away. 'I do despair,' she admitted softly. 'When I think what happened to José, I dread what will happen to Maria.

Each time she turns up here, I find myself breathing a sigh of relief that she's still alive, still able to grub around in the gutter. It would take a miracle to rescue her from the streets.'

Peter nodded slowly. He had good reason to believe Maria should stand a chance in life. If it hadn't been for her, he would be dead. But I didn't see Tania's sadness reflected in his face. He looked angry. I wondered why.

He hobbled over and touched Maria's shoulder, making her jump up from her book.

'Maria, what do you want from life?' he demanded.

She was startled, but answered without hesitation.

'More than anything, I want to find out what happened to my brother José. Until then, I cannot rest in peace. That is why I am learning to read and write. I can find out where he is from the educated people. The people with power.'

'And what about the gang?'

'I want a proper home for them. Somewhere safe. Somewhere beautiful. Somewhere we don't have to grub around in dustbins for food. I want us all to be able to go to school and learn things and hear stories and make things. I want to...' She paused, searching for the word. 'I want to *play*.' She shrugged. 'But these are all dreams, Mister Peter. All dreams.'

Tania nodded and packed away her few bits of chalk into her bag to take home. Peter started.

'Maria! I nearly forgot! What we've trailed all the way up here to tell you!'

Tania interrupted. 'Talk all you like, but I have to go out. Marco, will you lock the doors? I have a spare key. Leave this one next door with Pastor Carrios.

Senhor Clark, I am pleased to have met you. Maybe we will meet again.'

'I hope so,' said Peter sincerely. Tania gave Maria a brief hug, touched my cheek and left.

'You men!' teased Maria. 'One touch from a pretty woman and you go soft. Your important business, Senhor?'

Peter and I jerked out of watching Tania's departure. I don't know what was running through his mind, but I was wondering if my mother would have touched me like that, all her love distilled into a brush with one finger.

Peter tore his eyes away.

'Mmmm, yes. Yes. Look, Maria, you were right about Luiz. He's up to no good. We heard him planning to take over the gang – he wants to turn them all into drug couriers.'

'Over my dead body!' snapped Maria, suddenly serious.

'That's what we came to warn you about – Luiz is probably lying in wait for you. He knows he has to get rid of you before he can take over the gang. He'll have reinforcements from the dealer he's mixing with. If you go back to the building site, you won't stand a chance.'

'He's telling the truth, Maria,' I nodded.

'But I can't just abandon the gang!' said Maria, very pale now. 'I have to go back to them and keep them out of Luiz's hands. Ah, the...!' Peter thankfully didn't understand the descriptions she was spitting out. Any business school teaching language like that would be struck off. 'He would lead them into terrible danger. My Isabella! Joca! Roberto! I can't just leave them!'

I looked away. I had been so intent on warning

Maria, I hadn't thought beyond the immediate future of trying to keep her safe. But I realised that Peter had been one step ahead of me. He must have understood the way her mind works.

'You don't have to abandon the gang. Will you listen to me? I think I may have a plan that will sort out Luiz once and for all.' He went to the door and shouted, 'Chico! Come in and listen!'

8

'*Pssst*! Bebe! This way!'

Bebe, the little girl in the yellow dress who had served Peter his breakfast, turned in surprise. She, Zeze, Ze Pequeno, Caju and Junior were just about to duck through the hole in the wire fence around the building site to go home. They had their arms – and mouths – full of their pickings from the market, a bumper find today that they couldn't wait to show Maria. Then Bebe heard the whisper.

'This way!'

Catching sight of me beckoning furiously from the shadow of a doorway, Bebe pulled the others with her and they ducked into the hiding place, Ze Pequeno giggling and thumping me hard. I caught his fists.

'Sssh!' I whispered. 'Little ones, we are in great danger. Luiz wants to betray Maria and us to the drug barons. Will you help me save her?'

'Of course!' they whispered back, their eyes wide in the shadows. I put my arms round their shoulders. 'The Inglese – Peter – he has a plan. Listen carefully and tell me if you think you can do what he wants.'

'Hey! Joca! Roberto! Gilvam!' Joca and Gilvam turned quickly to stand back to back in a reflex defensive action, each of them peering in a different direction down the alleyway. The voice called again from an old wooden hut. 'It's only me, Chico! Quick – get yourselves down here, will you? It's going to be all fun and games back at home – are you fit for a fight? Listen, while I tell you Mister Peter's plan...'

A man limped cautiously across the building site and disappeared into the corner where the digger, the concrete mixer and the huge yellow bulldozer had been abandoned many months ago.

Not long afterwards, small figures could be seen scurrying on to the building site then vanishing into the landscape. There was a ripping noise, a splashing of water, a very soft chink of ceramic. From the far end of the site came a muffled sound of metal on metal, the occasional curse, the sound of an engine firing momentarily to life, and a satisfied grunt. Then there was only the late afternoon silence.

So it was that when Luiz ducked through the wire fence and gestured impatiently for the two thugs, one fat, one spotty, to do the same, the building site seemed deserted.

'They're not back yet,' he hissed. 'All the better for us, eh? There's the car. You'd better wait behind it, out of sight.'

'Who's giving the orders here, kid?' growled the fat man, furious at getting his snazzy clothes caught on the wire fence. 'We'll decide where we wait. You just do the job as quick as you can. Then we'll tidy up and get out of this dump. I've got a drink waiting.'

The two of them propped themselves against the side of the car, idly scratching its rusty surface with their knives, and smoking sagging cigarettes. Luiz hovered nervously by the bonnet, glancing around him, clutching a cigarette in one hand and chewing the nails of the other. Minutes passed.

'Look, when's this chick going to get back?' snarled the spotty man. 'I got better things to do than wait round here. Stood you up, has she?' He sniggered unpleasantly. Luiz swallowed and ran his finger round the neck of his T-shirt.

'She'll be here soon. Must've got held up.'

'Well, let's hope she's here soon – for your sake, kid. The Fox don't take kindly to his men wasting their time. He tends to... *punish* time wasters.' The two of them leered at Luiz.

'She'll be here, I tell you. She makes sure the kids get something to eat and get washed before they sleep.'

'What is this? Nursery school?'

'It'll be different when I'm in charge! I'll toughen them up!' shouted Luiz.

'Oh really, Luiz? And how do you propose to do that?' And out of nowhere, Maria was standing in front of him, smiling a lazy, dangerous smile.

'H... how did you get here? I never heard you come!' stammered Luiz, taken aback.

'Oh? I got the impression you were expecting me,' said Maria.

'N... N... no, not at all.' Luiz swallowed, glanced desperately at the side of the car where the men were hiding, and tried a feeble smile. It didn't suit him. 'Look, Maria, there's something I want to tell you. Can we go over there and talk?' Luiz pointed to a heap of dug-up earth.

'I'd love to talk to you, Luiz, but...' Maria raised her eyebrows innocently, 'what about your friends behind the car? Don't they want to come too? Mind you, if I had a face as ugly as theirs, I think I'd try to stay out of sight as well.' The two thugs gaped, then swung out angrily.

'I've had enough of this!' shouted the fat one. 'Keeping us hanging around for ages, then all this wise-talk – let's finish her off. Little bitch deserves it.'

The two of them pushed Luiz out of the way, leaving him flat on his face on the dusty ground, then charged at Maria, knives out.

Maria whipped round and bolted towards the building debris like an arrow from a bow. She knew the layout of the strewn equipment perfectly and dodged without hesitation over and around the familiar heaps of sand, the piles of sacks and the odd planks. The two men in their tight city trousers lost valuable seconds each time they came across a new obstacle. Maria wove in and out until she had led them into the very thick of the building site, stopping suddenly with a cry by a stack of long drainage pipes.

'Little so and so's done her ankle in!' panted the spotty one. 'Let's get her!' With teeth bared, they dived down the pile of sand towards her, as Maria clutched her ankle and stared at them in what looked like terror. 'Your time has come, lady. Say your prayers!' Fatty raised his knife ready to stab her, but a fierce howl echoed out of the pipes.

'What the—?' gasped Spotty.

Like deadly snakes out of their holes, my team of five scrambled out over the pipes. Each of us was brandishing a knife, broken bottle or razor blade. With a yelp, the two men turned on their heels and ran like mad back the way they thought they'd come, with me, Maria (her ankle miraculously unhurt) and the little ones close behind them. We herded them further into the site, like a pack of wolves chasing its prey. We skirted an enormous heap of bricks. I shouted, 'Now!' and the others veered away, leaving me alone in pursuit.

'Only one now, Regi!' panted Fatty. 'What say we do him?'

They turned on me and started to swipe at me. Fatty's knife caught me on the shoulder as I ducked, but I jumped up again somehow and kicked the knife out of Spotty's hand. 'You leave our gang alone, Mister,' I said through clenched teeth, and raising my voice, called, '*Chico*!'

'Not another of them!' groaned Spotty. There was a whoop of sheer joy from above as the heap of bricks in front of them came crashing down, driving them backwards in a choking cloud of dust. Over the bricks came Chico with his team of three, careering down with no thought of tripping on the rubble. They charged the two men, who turned in panic and were chased by the screeching boys behind them round another dirt pile. Before the men could stop themselves, they had run headlong into a wide expanse of what looked like mud. Spotty looked down at his smart clothes in horror.

'Cement!' he shrieked. 'Get me out of here! You little brats! You'll pay for this!' But instead of helping them out, Chico, Gilvam and the others picked up handfuls of cement and pelted it at the two thugs. The wet cement hit them smack on their outfits with satisfying squelches.

'Get off! Get off!' they squealed.

At a whistle from far away, Chico's companions pelted their last handfuls, and with shouts of laughter, scurried out of sight. Chico paused, then began:

'Oh, Senhor – your smart clothes! Oh, what will your lady friends say? What will your mothers say when you put them in the wash? "Oh, Spotty! What has happened to your lovely jacket?" "Fatso, my sweet, just look at your handsome tie!"'

Chico acted out the distraught mothers as if totally lost in his own drama, appearing not to notice that the two men were clambering out of the cement and lumbering heavily towards him, their faces grim. They lunged at him while he was in mid-scene, but Chico must have been more aware of them than they had thought. He catapulted himself between them in a neat forward roll and danced off towards the far end of the site, just fast enough to stay ahead of them, but slow enough to make it look as though they might catch up with him. The two men were furious now and their anger gave them a speed that Chico hadn't expected. As he pirouetted on a breezeblock, Spotty reached out as he ran and grabbed him by the arm.

'Think you can get away with fooling with us, do you?' he snarled, and smacked Chico round the head in a practised brutal swipe. The two of them started laying into him viciously. Chico curled on the ground and didn't let out a sound, but then a shout came from ahead.

'*Let him go!*' Out of nowhere streaked Maria, pelting headlong at Spotty, knocking him flat with the force of her speed. She laid into him with her fists while Chico did his best to keep Fatty and his knife away from her. The two children were fitter by far, and used to dirty fights, but the men were stronger and Maria knew they couldn't hold out for long. Then when Luiz ran in, Maria knew they were outnumbered. 'Peter!' she screamed.

From just behind a pile of earth there was a guttural cough as an engine spluttered into life, then to the thugs' horror, an enormous bulldozer trundled round the corner and drove straight at them.

Maria and Chico took advantage of the men's shock, wrenched themselves free and dived towards the machine, while the three would-be drug-pushers took one look at the monster bearing down on them with its huge scoop and its sharp teeth, and ran. But they weren't fast enough. The sharp scoop caught the backs of their knees painfully and tripped them up. Before they could scramble to their feet, they found themselves scooped up then hoisted up impossibly high as the great vehicle, still driving along as fast as it would go, bumped and banged them around the site. Luiz was bumped up above the edge and caught sight of the driver – or rather, the drivers. Peter held the controls, a look of steady concentration on his face, and crammed into the cab around him was the whole gang, cheering, hooting and waving.

The bulldozer jerked to a halt at the perimeter fence, its scoop still high up in the air. Too bruised and sick to move, the three clung there while the gang bailed out and gathered round the vehicle. It was Maria who spoke above the noise of the engine.

'If you men dare to come back here, there will be more of the same. Leave us alone, and we will leave you alone. Luiz...' she paused. 'For myself, I forgive you. For what you wanted to do to my children, I have to tell you, do not come back, or it will not go well with you. Now get out.'

Peter pushed the lever and the scoop tipped the three out on the far side of the fence like three grubby ragdolls. Too shaken even to look back, they staggered to their feet and stumbled away into the city.

Peter switched off the engine. There was a moment's silence, then cheers broke out as the gang hugged each other and Peter.

'We did it!' shouted Maria, her arm over Peter's shoulders. 'We need to celebrate! Get that machine put back, let's get your shoulder seen to, Marco. The rest of you – find all the food we've got – let's party!'

I toned the dance music down to soft arpeggios on my battered old guitar, which rested comfortably enough against my hurt shoulder. Peter lay against the car, his arms around the shoulders of Caju and Zeze who were curled up against him, too tired to carry on dancing. Bebe was on his knee, for once managing not to put her hands all over his face. Peter had laughed and sung along to the music and clapped as Maria and Chico danced their wild swirling sambas at double-speed, and he had eaten and drunk the pickings with none of the hesitation he had shown earlier. Now a shadow passed over his face.

'Shall I get your painkillers?' I murmured over Isabella's sleepy body hunched up against my leg.

'It's not my ankle hurting this time, ' he said.

Maria flopped down beside Peter, pulling Chico down with her and ruffling his hair. A stillness fell on us all. Maria broke it.

'A marvellous feast, Bebe. The stallholders were kind to you today. You worked hard. I think Mister Peter will not eat as well in his fine hotel!'

Peter smiled, a little ruefully. 'I won't have chance to try any more hotel food, anyway. My plane leaves in the morning. I'll be back in England by nightfall.'

I struck a wrong note. I had got so used to him being here, being part of us, that I had forgotten he had to leave us. That he should have left us already.

Ze Pequeno touched his arm and looked up into his face. 'Don't go, Mister Peter – stay with us.'

Bebe wailed and flung her arms round him like the baby she was.

'Don't be silly, Ze,' said Maria, pulling Bebe away on to her own lap and enduring her kicks of protest. 'Mister Peter doesn't belong here with us. He has a home in England, a fine house, I should think, not a rusty old car. He has money, don't forget. Just because he has been stuck with us for two days doesn't mean he has lost all his money. And besides, he has his—'

'*Important business*,' cut in Peter before she could say it. 'Yes, I have to go back. This is your home, your country, your life, not mine. But... I want to thank you for letting me share it all with you. I... won't forget you.'

The firelight danced over our faces. Brown skin, black skin, black mops of hair, dark eyes shining in the darkness at his pale skin, blue eyes, fair hair. Thirteen children, skinny and stinking with disease, wheezing with asthma, scratching boils that refused to heal, skin that would always be scarred, their eyes older than the city itself; and him, strong and rich and well-nourished...

'I don't know how to say this,' he continued, so quietly we could hardly hear him. 'Before I met you I thought my life was sorted and full and real. Then you bunch of good Samaritans pulled me out of the gutter and showed me what real love is about. And I don't think my life can ever be quite the same again. You, Chico, always smiling even in the darkest times... You, Marco, with your sharp eyes and your longing for something I can't even begin to guess at... And Maria, with your courage and love and life... I won't forget you.'

We sat in silence by the glowing embers long into the city night while the children tossed and muttered in our arms.

9

It wasn't until much later that we found out how this part of the story went. It's hard to picture it happening over there in that cold country so far from our own. But I think it must have been something like this.

I see a wood-panelled office with soft rugs on the floor and framed pictures on the walls. It is in the most expensive part of London. A view from the window of tall buildings, cathedrals and a tall clocktower. A smell of coffee.

A man in an expensive suit is sitting at a computer tapping in a row of figures. It is Peter. He is hard at work and concentrating on the job in hand.

The intercom buzzes discreetly.

'It's Mr Lopez from Eurocom for you, Mr Clark,' purred Peter's secretary. 'Will you see him now?'

Peter smiled. Enrico Lopez, his South American counterpart? 'Certainly! Yes, show him in!' As the businessman was ushered into his luxuriously furnished office, Peter leapt to his feet and welcomed him warmly. Enrico Lopez chuckled and sat down in the leather armchair.

'So, Peter, you are none the worse for your little escapade, eh? Tell me, wicked one, where did you get to for the last days of the conference? We missed you so very much. A girl, was it?'

Peter laughed. 'You could say so!'

'I thought as much! This was delivered to our office by hand a few days after your departure.' Enrico passed Peter a crumpled envelope. Peter snatched it from him in surprised delight. On the front 'Mister Peter Clarc' was written in pencil.

'I'll... open it later,' he said, putting it in his breast pocket, where it seemed to be shouting to be read until Enrico had done his business and left.

The moment he had been passed on to the secretary, Peter pulled out the envelope and tore it open. The letter inside was written on a single sheet of cheap notepaper in laboriously formed handwriting. He read it, a slow grin spreading across his face.

Mister Peter
thank you for your help the gang is a little safer now
Marco goes better school is good. tania helps me
write this letter. she tak it to your offise. She say hello
Go with God. Maria.

'Love letters from South America, Mr Clark?' asked his secretary, as she peeked round the door. Her varnished fingernails tapped on the doorframe. Peter raised his eyebrows and she coughed in embarrassment, placed a china cup of coffee on his desk and disappeared, her silk shirt whispering expensively around her.

Peter knew she was keen on him, but the feeling was scarcely mutual. His thoughts flew back to a very different girl.

He pictured Maria, grubby and brave, struggling to write that note to him, determined to pay a debt of thanks to him, to show how much he meant to them all. He thought of Tania, the dedicated teacher, ready to grab her revolver at the first sign of trouble. He thought of Marco, recovering quietly and uncomplainingly from that knife-wound – how much fuss had Peter made about his far less-seriously injured ankle! And Chico, bouncing around them all, always cheerful, always generous, always cheeky. They seemed so far away from that oak-panelled office with its thick carpet.

The coffee tasted of bitter pond water as he remembered that vivid picnic in the park with Rodrigo and the two boys. Peter was seized with a sudden pang of frustration. He folded the letter into his wallet and pulled on his warm woollen coat.

'I'm going out for a bit,' he told the secretary. 'If anyone calls, tell them I'll ring back.'

'But Mr Clark! You're down to see the Directors in twenty minutes!' bleated the secretary.

'Tell them I'll be late,' he called over his shoulder as he disappeared into the lift, leaving the secretary twittering about how Mr Clark had changed since his last trip to South America – all that nonsense about recycling! Changing the brand of coffee they bought! Digging out the company policies on equality and haranguing the Board until they were altered! He simply wasn't as nicely reliable and predictable as he used to be.

Peter strode off down the city street, pounding past mums with babies in strollers, his hands thrust deep in his pockets, partly because of the bitter cold and partly because he was seething with a range of emotions that he didn't know what to do with. He went on, hardly noticing where he was, determined just to vent some of the fierce anger and guilt that was coursing through him. The words of Maria's note came back to him. 'Go with God' she'd written, just as she always said to the children before they set out into the dangers of the city. Well, here was a church, whose door opened up when he pushed it. Why not go in here and work out what exactly was bugging him?

It was quiet inside, of course. Cool and dry, clean and peaceful. A far cry from the filthy dumps of the city where his children rummaged for food. Totally alien from the shimmeringly hot streets where Chico kicked a football. As big as Tania's schoolroom, but with a carpet, seats, glistenings of gold and silver, rich reds and blues, Bibles neatly stacked in the pews; not the bleak white barn with no money for extras like books. Peter snorted in frustration. This wasn't the place to sort through his crisis: there was no link with Maria's gang here. He turned to leave, but as he did so, a head popped up from behind a pew.

'Hello!' It was a little boy, about eight years old, with a shock of dark hair and freckles.

'Hello,' replied Peter. He thought of asking why the boy wasn't at school, but it seemed such a tedious, patronising question – and what business of his was it anyway? He sat down in the nearest pew. But the boy read his thoughts.

'I'm on half term holiday,' he said, clambering over the pew to sit next to Peter. 'I'm waiting until Daddy's finished, then we're going to the park.'

'Your daddy's here?' asked Peter, looking around.

'Yes, he's looking at the central heating. It smells.'

'Ah.'

'Are you waiting to see Daddy too?'

'No, I just came in here...' Peter stopped. He had been about to fob the boy off with some lie about coming in to get warm, but his directness somehow reminded Peter of the faraway children who were so much on his mind. He turned to the boy.

'I feel very sad because my best friends live a long way away.'

The boy thought. 'Why don't you go and see them?' he asked.

'Because it's too far for a visit.'

'You could go and live with them.'

Peter looked at him. The boy waited politely. A few months ago, Peter would have said, 'Oh you're too young to understand.' But the boy's words had lit a tiny light at the back of his mind, the first light he'd felt since he had come back to England. He was about to speak when the door banged. He turned.

'Hello,' said the newcomer in a kind voice. 'I hope my son hasn't annoyed you. I was just investigating the cause of the smell my congregation have been complaining of, and I think I've located a dead mouse under the grating. But if I can be of any help...?'

The newcomer, a dark-haired man with infinitely kind eyes, peered at Peter anxiously. Peter was going to shake his head and leave, but something about the thought of a dead mouse rotting beneath the floor forged a tenuous link with the filth of the city that was so much on his mind, and the kind eyes of the vicar showed nothing but an straightforward readiness to help.

So he stayed where he was, the small boy beside him, and, staring straight ahead, said exactly what was on his mind. He told the story of his meeting with the street children, their rescue of him, the day they spent together, Doctor Gilberto, Tania, the fight at the building site.

'And since I came home, everything has changed. I used to be happy in my job – I mean, it seemed so important. But now it seems so empty, so meaningless. I sit in my office, but in my mind I just see the street kids struggling for existence, one step ahead of the drug dealers and the death squads. They could be dead now, and I'd never know. I've got so much here – a good job, a huge house, sports clubs, restaurants – the whole of London at my fingertips, and they have so little. And they saved my life. I can't forget that. And Rodrigo spent his last coins on me. I have so much and they have nothing. And they laugh with their poverty, and I'm wretched with all my money. All they want is a home where Maria and the others can be safe, can go to school. They gave me all they had, and it's left me feeling this incredible burden of guilt so that I can't enjoy anything any more. I think about them all the time. If I could pay off my debt to them, perhaps I'd feel more content. But what can I give them in return? Nothing. They're thousands of miles away. I don't know what to do.'

The vicar polished his spectacles thoughtfully.

'Do you mind me asking – have you any family ties?'

'Nothing that counts.'

'And you are comfortably off as far as money is concerned?'

'I have more than I know what to do with. My job pays well, and I don't have much time to spend it, so, yes, I've got a fair amount.'

'So you have no ties to keep you here, and you have enough money to be reckless.'

Peter stared at the dark-haired man. 'What are you saying?'

'Think about it,' said the vicar. 'You are not at peace. And forgive me for saying this, but I don't believe you will be at peace until you have obeyed what God has laid on your heart.'

'Are you suggesting I just leave everything and go back to South America? It's impossible! My job! My house! My friends! I couldn't possibly do that... I couldn't... Could I?'

Peter stood up. Go there for good? The thought was ridiculous. It would be so irresponsible – giving up his regular job for who knows what, throwing himself into an alien culture, with nothing but a basic knowledge of the language and the friendship of thirteen youngsters! It would mean giving up his whole life for them – were they worth it?

And as soon as he'd framed the question, Peter felt deeply ashamed. Worth it? Of course they were worth it! And with that clear in his mind, the rest fell into place as if he had suddenly stepped on to the main road after blundering about in the filth of the *favela*. It was so simple. He would go back to South America and buy a home for Maria and the others. He blinked.

'Thank you,' he said.

The vicar shrugged.

'Must get back to the mouse.' He stood and laid a tentative hand on Peter's shoulder. 'May God bless you in what you've decided to do. Come on, Harry.'

'Go with God,' replied Peter softly, and went out into the street, his mind working at double speed, planning, plotting, glowingly alive at the thought of returning to South America, to Maria, to Marco and Chico, to Tania.

'You are off your trolley, Clark!' shouted his boss, when he handed in his notice and told her why he was leaving. 'I won't accept this resignation! The company needs you! You can't throw your life away in the back streets of some ghastly South American ghetto! Your skills are here, at the computer console, making important decisions!'

'Making more money for the firm, you mean?' said Peter. 'I've tried to explain, I can't do that any more. This project is more than computer consoles – it's about real people, about life and death.'

'Don't be so melodramatic, Clark,' blared the boss. 'It's simply not done. This is totally absurd, throwing away all you've been trained for. What a waste of an education! I beg you, don't do it!'

The secretary sniffed and looked at him as if he had come into the office with no clothes on. What a lucky escape she'd had, she thought, and applied herself to tidying the office ready for the new manager.

'Peter, darling, you must be mad!' said his friends. 'I mean, South America! If you're feeling restless, why not just take a year out? Travel! See the world! Enjoy yourself for a bit! Don't go burying yourself alive in some hellhole. How can we come for holidays with you in a slum like that?' they joked.

The bank manager looked very grave.

'Of course the decision lies entirely with you, Mr Clark, but it is my responsibility to point out to you that transferring your entire savings to a foreign account will pose some insurmountable problems and will almost certainly work out to your disadvantage.'

'*Why* do you want a visa for this country? *How* long do you intend to stay there? Is it business or pleasure?' they demanded at the embassy, presenting him with enough forms to justify the deforestation of several acres of tropical jungle.

'*Why* do you want export licences for all this furniture and sports equipment?' they asked in the interrogation at Customs and Excise.

And on and on. Peter found it hard to believe that such a simple step – moving to another country to help a bunch of kids get a life – could produce so much paperwork, bureaucracy and general bewilderment amongst those on this side. He ploughed through it all, even the most boring, pointless forms, helped on by the conviction that he was doing the right thing. Most of the time this certainty helped him stay calm even in the face of official obstruction. Only once did he lose his patience with bureaucracy. After Peter had waited in a queue for two hours, the clerk behind the computer shook his head.

'Oh no, sir, I can't give you that certificate. Your form EP-769 had no signature in box 39f. No, naturally I've shredded the original. Here's a new one to fill in, with four extra pages for travellers outside the EU. Well, if you can complete it within the week, it might go through the system by next month. But we are very short-staffed at the moment. Shall we say, come back in ten weeks and we'll see what we can do?'

Peter's subsequent explosion brought the whole office to a standstill for a full minute. The clerk turned pale, visibly shook as he scribbled on a piece of paper and thrust the certificate into Peter's hand.

'That will do nicely, sir,' he stammered. 'Bon voyage.'

Peter bulldozed his way through the forms, through the tangle of travel regulations and financial conundrums, driven on by the thought of meeting Maria down at the building site, seeing her face light up as he told her what he'd come to do, sharing out sweets and treats with the children, taking them all to safety...

At last the waiting was over; the forms were stamped and all the goodbyes were said. The flight across half a world seemed endless, the meals tasteless, the film about two blond children and their puppy unbearably cute. The moment came when he stepped out into the city, carrying only a light holdall with basic essentials in, and set out in search of his children.

It was six months since he had last been in the city. He took a taxi as close to the *favela* as it was prepared to take him, then got out and, keeping a tight hold on his wallet, walked down the narrow paths, following his map and his memory.

Here was the square where they had found Rodrigo being beaten up.

Here was the alley where Chico had lurked on that last night, waiting for the boys.

Here was the gap in the fence that led on to the building site.

And here... here was the car.

'Maria?' he called, softly. There was no reply. Well, that was to be expected. How could he have got word to her that he was coming? They must all be out doing the rounds of the dumps and dustbins, or snatching a few hours at Tania's school.

He peered under the car, expecting to see the familiar clutter of boxes, guitars, blankets and bags that the children stored there. But it was empty. There was no sign of life.

The gang didn't live there any more.

For the first time since his decision in the church, Peter found his nerve breaking. He hadn't thought of this possibility – that the gang had moved somewhere he would never find them. What if he'd given up everything... for nothing? Then something caught his eye.

What were those holes in the roof of the car?

'Hey! You! Get out of here! This is private property!' came a shout. A stocky man was lumbering towards him, a truncheon thumping against the palm of his hand. 'I suppose you're working out how much you could get for these building materials if you was to come one night with a big lorry and take the lot, eh? Eh?' He thrust his chin out and stared at Peter.

'No, I was wondering what happened to the children who used to live here. I don't suppose you know?'

'What's it worth?'

Peter peeled off a banknote and stuffed it in the man's sweaty hand.

'Now, what happened to them?'

'I gets wind of them a while ago, from a certain contact I have on the streets, who had a score to settle with these kids. I watched out for them. Goodness knows how long they'd been hiding out down here, robbing and stealing. So I tells the people who wants to hear about filth like that. Know what I mean? Can't have vermin like that round my patch. Next night, along comes this big van. I hear machine guns. In the morning, there's no kids left. One problem out of the way, eh? I cleans out their hidey hole, sells off the junk underneath and all's right and tight. Must mend that hole in the fence, though. What's up, Senhor? You look like you've seen a ghost.'

10

Peter said nothing, turned, and walked back through the building site.

Out through the hole in the fence.

Back down the paths.

The shock was too much to put into conscious thought.

Marco's words about Maria's lost brother José echoed in his head: 'I think he was shot down like a dog.'

The death squads. The disappearing ones. His children.

The fire of anger against injustice that had begun to burn in him all those months ago flared up in an all-consuming blaze.

'*NO*!'

Peter's shout that rang around the rooftops startled the passers-by. But Peter himself was past caring. If his children were dead, where was the point in going on?

Common sense told him to find out more. Who could he ask? Who would know about his children?

Of course! Tania! Could he remember the way to her school?

Storming through the streets, up the hills, driven by

ferocious instinct and a flaming fury against the murderers, he pitched up at the school building and hammered on the door. Silence.

He beat against it again, tried to open it, thumped again.

'Tania! Tania Miguele! If you're in there, open the door!'

Silence.

The sun beat down. Peter sank slowly against the wall until he was slumped on the ground, his head between his legs.

'Oh God, where were you when they shot my children?'

Silence.

Then came the tiny sound of a key being turned in the lock. The door was pushed open a crack, and someone inside gave a gasp of astonishment.

'Peter Clark! Senhor!'

Peter looked up and saw Tania beckoning him frantically into the school. He got up, followed her in and watched her lock and bolt the door behind them. She turned to face him. He saw she was as beautiful as he'd remembered, but strained and exhausted.

'They shot the children,' he said.

'What?'

'They came to the building site. They shot them. Maria, Marco, little Chico, and all the others.' Peter was too strung up to care; his voice broke. 'They shot my children and I'm too late to help them!'

Tania had her arm around his shoulders as he sat slumped over a bench, racked with sobs.

'No, no,' she was saying in distress. 'No, the children are alive. They're here, they're safe. They escaped.'

'They *what*?'

'They escaped!'

Peter looked at her, conscious not of the words she was saying but only of the warmth in her eyes pleading with him to understand.

'Maria! Come out! It's okay!'

And out we came.

Peter looked so different from the last time we had seen him. The ragged filthy suit had been replaced with a blue shirt and jeans. His hair was shiny, he was clean, and now, as he saw the stream of children erupting from the back room, his face was rigid with shock. Tania seemed to be hiding tears. Why would she cry when Peter was back?

Peter grabbed the children as they came flying at him, and hugged each one, until he was buried under a squealing, wriggling mass of small ones.

'Mister Peter!' grinned Chico, biffing him on the shoulder. 'Back for another fight, eh?'

I took Peter's hand in my two hands and clasped it, saying nothing. The strong warmth of his grip seemed to pour new courage into me after the nightmare of the last week. I felt the heavy load of responsibility ease. I was deeply glad to see him again. He paused in his struggle with the little ones and returned my tight clasp.

'Marco,' he said.

And waiting behind the throng, watching in amusement was Maria.

'So, Mister Peter,' she said quietly, when the rabble had settled down to a giggle of contentment. 'More important business in our country?'

Peter gazed at her across the curly heads of the

youngsters he was hugging.

'Possibly the most important business I've ever planned in my life,' he said. 'But first, tell me, what happened to you?'

I had heard the van coming.

Nothing ever came on to the building site, let alone in the middle of the night. I was lying awake as usual, making pictures of imaginary parents in my head, when the rumbling engine and hiss of brakes jolted me upright.

'Maria!' I called through my teeth as I shook the boys awake.

We could all hear the rusty gates being forced open at the far end of the site.

Maria's white face rose up at the window.

'All of you. Take nothing. Follow me – and run. Marco?'

I understood I would be last and check they had all got away.

The engine revved up. It sounded so near.

I pushed each of the little ones out of the windows. Never had I been so glad that they would obey Maria without pausing to question her. Straight from sleep to a stumbling run through the pipes and round the back of the earth piles in Maria's shadow they went without a word.

The rumbling was getting nearer. The van was on the site and coming straight for us.

'Come *on*, Marco!'

Chico was beckoning madly from the pipes as I shoved Roberto out and slid down to the ground myself. Together we pulled him into the relative safety of the shadows and ran, dragging him along between us, as we had never run before.

We heard the machine guns behind us through Roberto's stifled sobs.

It was the hour after dawn when Doctor Gilberto found us on the doorstep of his clinic.

'What on earth...? Maria, what have you done this time?'

Then he realised that Isabella was crying in Maria's arms, and that Maria's face was grey and set. He fumbled with the key.

'Don't just stand there – come in off the street. How long have you been here? No, leave the shutters shut. No one must see you here. What happened?'

Maria was busy calming Isabella and Bebe. Gilvam was throwing up in a corner. Zeze and Roberto had collapsed on to the floor and were rocking backwards and forwards, their eyes glazed over while Chico stroked their shoulders and talked nonsense at them. So I told the doctor the facts over Caju's head that was buried in my neck. The doctor thrust his face into his hands.

'Stay here. Don't open the door for anyone. The death squads may just be out for any street kids. But with your reputation, you have many enemies in the streets and someone could have deliberately betrayed you. They may have been looking for you in particular. Better that they think you're dead.'

He was only gone a few minutes, and returned with bread and milk, which he made us eat. I thought I would never feel hungry again, but forced it down to please him. The little ones started to look less petrified, even if Caju was still shaking.

'My patients will be arriving soon,' said the doctor. 'I have nowhere for you to hide. I don't think the fat wealthy ladies of the city will appreciate you watching me examine their ingrown toenails. Go now, before there are too many people on the streets. Don't go anywhere near your old home ever again. Go to... go to Tania. Tell her I'll help her sort something out for you. I'll come by tonight. Quick now, run, before the streets fill.'

His voice was hard but there was worry in his eyes. He patted Maria's shoulder. 'Courage, little one.'

For the first time since she had finished her wild mourning for her brother, I saw Maria's eyes filling up with tears. Her shoulders sagged and she rubbed her face with a weary filthy hand.

'I can't do any more,' she whispered. 'I can't keep them safe. The Fox will pick them off one by one. They're all going to die.'

The doctor squatted down in front of her and held her shoulders. His voice was soft and strong. 'And where is Jesus in this?' he asked. She shrugged, the tears running down her cheeks.

'Has it just been a game up to now, then?' he demanded. 'Believing God will look after you? You think that now you've reached rock bottom, he'll laugh in your face and leave you to fend for yourselves?' He gave her shoulders a shake. 'He never said it would be easy, Maria. But he's your hiding place, your rock and your rescuer, and he will never let you down.'

'They shot at us!' she stammered. 'They would have killed us all!'

'But they *didn't*. You're *here*. You're *alive*.'

'For the moment! But for how long? How can he

rescue us from this?' she cried out, staring up at him in desperation. 'There is no escape! There is nowhere left to run!'

'I don't know,' replied the doctor. 'But he'll find a way that will go beyond your wildest dreams. Trust him. Go to Tania.'

She drew herself up, beckoned sharply to the gang, dragged Bebe and Isabella up by the hand and strode out without another word.

As I went out behind the others, he held me back a moment. 'Stick together, Marco,' he muttered, the distress carving deep furrows in his forehead. 'She needs you. She would be lost without you. Whatever you do, stay together.'

'So,' I told Peter over the top of Gilvam and Zeze's heads, 'we came up here to Tania and she hid us in her back rooms. The doctor brings food each night. But we're eating them out of house and home!'

'The authorities cannot fail to discover soon that they are here, Peter,' said Tania. 'And then they would be happier on the streets – they would all be sent to different orphanages.'

Zeze scowled. 'I spit on the authorities.''

'Not in here you don't,' snapped Maria.

Zeze brandished his knife. 'Let them try to split us up! I'll kill them first!'

I took his knife from him and he bit my hand. I slapped him. He started to whine like a baby. Bebe copied him out of habit. Junior had wet himself again. I saw Maria start shivering. I hadn't slept for a week and my stomach seemed permanently cramped and aching. We were all on edge, ready to jump down each other's throats. Poor Tania was out of her depth.

Peter didn't look as distressed at our nervousness as I thought he should have done. In fact he grinned, and pulled Bebe on to one knee and Zeze on to the other, where they instantly shut up.

'I asked you a long time ago, Maria, what you wanted from life,' he said.

'I remember,' she nodded.

'It was in this schoolroom,' said Tania. 'You didn't ask for much, Maria. Just a safe home, education, that's all.'

'And my brother.'

'After the last week, I'd settle for just a safe home,' I said. The gang wriggled in a little closer to each other, the memory of that night of machine guns and silent desperate flight just a little too fresh in our minds. Junior shivered.

Peter held the children a little closer. 'I know,' he murmured.

It was at that point that I knew there was something he wasn't telling us. His eyes met mine across the group and I could tell he was holding something back for later. I nodded imperceptibly, all the time conscious of a growing feeling of relief, as if Peter was lifting a huge pack off my back. At this subtle reassurance that he had other plans for us than separate orphanages, I felt the rope of tension that had been a part of me for so long begin to unravel. I felt very tired.

'To bed, children,' said Maria. She swapped a glance with me. We had both seen there was something to discuss without the little ones.

11

We put the children to bed on the floor of the school, not without a fight. Since the escape, they had become more and more disobedient. It took me twenty minutes to calm Roberto's cackling and thrashing fit down to a level that wouldn't keep them all awake. It was even more difficult than normal to take the time to hug him through the sobs that follow each outburst, but eventually he collapsed into something that might have been sleep. Maria finished praying with Bebe, the only way we had found to make the little girl feel safe enough to sleep. Chico got to the end of Zeze's story, adding a pair of real leather football boots to the riches the fictional boy possessed.

Then Maria, Chico and I went to join Peter in the back room. We didn't mean to sneak in, but silent movements are a hard habit to break – and we all had a clear view of Peter's arm across Tania's shoulder, their heads bent close together, before Chico called, 'Ohé, Mister Peter! Save your cuddling till later!'

Tania and Peter jumped apart as if they were teenagers caught by their strict parents. I was intrigued. It's hard to imagine your teacher having a life apart from her pupils, and I had never seen Tania in the company of a man before – except Doctor

Gilberto, of course, who is always so busy doctoring that he doesn't count. I had never seen Tania ruffled before, either. Scared, yes. But never embarrassed like she was now. I glanced at Maria to share the joke. To my surprise, there was a second's fleeting impression of shocked disappointment across her face, which vanished so quickly back into her normal watchful calm that I wondered if I had been mistaken.

'You can take that smirk off your face, young Marco,' grumbled Peter, as he shifted back his chair to make room for us in a circle.

'Mister Peter's found his lady love...' warbled Chico, enjoying Tania's dull red blush.

'Shut up, Chico,' ordered Maria. 'There are more important things to talk about, aren't there, Senhor? Perhaps *you* can persuade Tania to let us move on. She says it's still too dangerous for us to be seen on the streets.'

'Word got around about the run-in with The Fox and Luiz,' said Tania in a weary voice. She had explained this to us so many times before. 'They are now laughed at wherever they go. Men like that take humiliation badly. The Fox has many friends in low places and high ones. Even if your home hadn't been destroyed, they would manage to get you somehow in revenge for your work with the bulldozer. And who else would have tried to have you murdered as you slept? They won't give up. You cannot go out yet. And soon they'll find you here...'

Maria turned to Peter in frustration. 'We can't stay here with Tania any longer. We're putting her in danger! There is no room. We can't hide forever! We can't do our work to earn our living: Tania and Anna can't do theirs with us underfoot all day. Tell her we have to go!'

Peter smiled. 'I agree,' he said, putting up a hand to shush Tania's exasperated protest. 'But you can't go back on the streets. Tania's right.'

'But where can we go?' said Maria. Her anger had given way to despair. I had never seen her so hopeless. 'Our parents are all dead now. If the raids haven't seen to them, the drugs have. Bebe's father died in prison of an overdose. Even Zeze's mother, the one who would welcome him home, then lock him away in the dark while she went out to work – we heard the other day that she's been knifed. She was the last of our parents alive. Even if we could persuade the little ones to go home, there are no homes to go to.'

Maria bit her lip. The last weeks had almost knocked the courage out of her. I put my arm about her shoulders, and for once, she didn't shrug me away. The hug wasn't wholly for her comfort anyway. I was imagining returning to my home. The memory of my father rose as vivid as a video before me. The last time I'd seen him, his fist dashing again and again into my mother's face, then turning on me before I ran. Even if he had been alive still, not knocked out of life in a drunken street brawl, I would never have returned to him. Even life on the streets was safer. We two would stick together. I hugged Maria tight.

Peter began to speak, so hesitantly that I didn't realise what he was saying at first.

'Suppose we could find a house in the country far away from all the fighting on the streets. Suppose it was big enough for the gang to live there until they were old enough to have homes of their own.

Somewhere safe. Would you come?'

We said nothing. The idea was so unexpected. Peter's face fell.

'If you don't think it's the answer...'

Then we all spoke at once.

'*A house in the country?*'

'*For all of us?*'

'*But how?*'

A flush of relief spread over Peter's face. 'For a minute, there, I thought you weren't interested.' He pulled a sheet of paper out of his briefcase. 'Take a look at that. What do you think?'

The picture on the estate agent's headed paper showed a blurred print of a building, a house, too indistinct for us to see much. Chico grabbed it and pored over it from all angles while I turned to Peter. My heart was thundering in my chest.

'What do you mean? How could this be ours? We couldn't live in a house. We're only street kids. We belong in the gutter.'

Peter leaned over and gripped my arm. He spoke with a fierce intensity. 'You don't belong in the gutter. You belong in a home with a family who will love you like you deserve to be loved. If it wasn't for you, I'd be dead now, don't you understand? I want to see to it that you get a chance for life as well. I can't give you your families back, but I could give you a safe home. You are worth more than the gutter, Marco, far more.'

Chico butted in. 'And look! There might be room for a football pitch round the side! We have to see this place, Marco.'

Maria hadn't even glanced at the paper. 'But what are you saying, Peter?' she asked. 'How could we live there or in any house on our own? How could we afford it?'

Peter looked down at the floor. 'If you could stand it, I was thinking of buying a place myself, but it might be a bit lonely. I'd need some company, people to help with the farm work, with restoring the buildings. I could use the gang, if you fancied coming to live with me.'

I looked at Maria. I could see what was going through her mind: a conflict between life on the streets, the only life she knew, and the security of a hideaway in the country, a place where the little ones could grow up in freedom and safety.

There was a long pause.

Peter said softly, 'We could go and see it tomorrow, then you could decide.'

Maria nodded slowly.

'To bed with the lot of you,' said Tania, standing up. 'It may be a holiday tomorrow, but I still have schoolwork to do.'

Chico caught the look that went between Tania and Peter and opened his mouth to make another comment. But I dragged him out of the room before he could speak. To my surprise, considering how much there was to think about that night, I fell asleep straight away and slept solidly until morning.

12

'Lazy lumps! Are you all still in bed?' came a man's voice from the schoolroom.

Ridiculous to still have that reflex that had my knife in my hand and my muscles tensed ready to run. Things were going to be different now. I forced myself to relax and walked round from the back of the school building to see who was there.

'Doctor Gilberto!'

'Marco! Still safe? Where is everyone?'

'Come and see who is here!' I was choosing my words to tell him about Peter, about the day's adventure ahead, about the house, when Chico burst round the corner, hooted, '*Doctor*!', grabbed his hand and, chattering at the top of his voice, dragged him full pelt round to where the others were loading up a bus with what seemed to be the contents of an entire supermarket. Peter looked up from a cardboard box filled with fizzy drinks, and his face broke into a grin at the sight of the doctor. He strode over to shake hands.

'Gilberto! Good to see you.'

'It's my day off from the clinic so I'd come up to check on the children. Ze Pequeno! Put that chocolate back in the box! Chico told me of your arrival. I didn't expect to see you again. How's the ankle?'

'Right as rain, thanks to you. Look, Gilberto, why don't you come too? Day in the country, it would do you a world of good.'

The doctor looked taken aback, then laughed. 'Well, why not?' he said. 'I hear you're house-hunting. You'll have your work cut out keeping those young tearaways in order in the bus – hired it for the day? Good idea. I'll come as crowd control.' He climbed in with the rest of us and sat next to a delighted Bebe, who threw herself on top of him and clung.

'Tania? Will you navigate?' Peter tossed her the map and pointed out the spot we were heading for. 'Quiet in the back! Everyone in? We're off!'

It's hard to explain how exciting it is to ride in a bus when you've never ridden in one before; or to leave the city when you've never seen the country before. The distances that would mean hours of sweaty walking up street after street flicked past as I sat and gazed down on the city, seeing it from a whole new angle. I was no longer down in the gutter; I was up above people's heads, looking down on them from my comfy seat.

The doctor did his best to keep the high spirits of the gang in reasonable check, but when things got altogether too rowdy for safety, it was Maria or Tania who got them back in their seats with a few snapped words.

As the cityscape gave way to fields and trees, the little ones became too busy pointing out new wonders out of the window to make any more trouble. The size and emptiness of the landscape made them nervous compared with the dense buildings and streets they were used to. And after an hour that went by as quickly as the flight of a mosquito, we came to the valley where the house was that we had come to see.

'Turn off here,' said Tania, as a rough track wound off on the right. I left my seat and came to sit next to her at the front to get a better view.

'Marco! You startled me!'

The gang gasped and giggled as we were bounced along the unmade road, which wound gently down the side of a hill, through some forest that was so thick it felt like night-time, breaking out on to a flat, open valley bottom, which was surrounded by rolling hills on all sides. There was a shallow blue river flowing through it, with white sandy beaches alongside it. Fields of green and yellow crops stretched out around the river. Right at the far end of the valley, well away from the river, and on slightly higher ground, stood a whitewashed farm with glowing flowerpot-coloured roofs. I could see a large sturdy barn, some smaller stables, an enormous tree casting shade across the farmyard and the farmhouse itself, huge and strong, standing like a fortress in the middle of the other buildings. The morning sun was caught in the sheltered valley and gave all the colours a rich fresh glow.

'This could be our home?' I whispered. Tania nodded, thrilled herself by the sight of so much beauty.

Peter drove slowly up the track, which followed the river up the valley and pulled into the farmyard. A flock of white doves fluttered up through the tree's branches and away, feather white against the blue sky. He let us out of the bus, and we clustered in the yard, quiet now in a hush of expectancy, out of our element of dusty streets and traffic. Maria hardly looked around, but walked deliberately to the farmhouse door and asked: 'So why are we waiting?'

Her voice was brusque to the point of rudeness. I wondered what this meant to her – how much it hurt to hand over the gang to Peter and his mad wonderful idea of giving us a home. And whether she was thinking the same as I was – who would be in charge now?

Peter unlocked the heavy wooden door and pushed it open to reveal dim stone floors and rough plastered walls, beams in dark wood and the smell of disuse.

'Off you go – go and explore it – see what you think!' said Peter. The little ones didn't need telling twice. They were off in a whirl of excitement. As Maria and I wandered with the three adults through the old house, we could hear the joyful noise echoing around the empty rooms. Shutters were thrown open and sunlight flooded the rooms, filling them with warmth and life. Children's voices, laughs and shrieks span through the still air like silver thread. Peter and Tania were full of plans:

'Imagine this as a dining room – a huge table in the middle, benches on either side. A fire in that huge fireplace on winter evenings.'

'Look at this kitchen! We could put armchairs around the stove, cushions on that windowseat. Fit a fridge in there, rip that old sink out and put in something usable...'

'This could be an office, a library maybe.'

'How about this living room? We could put a huge soft rug on the stone floor. Put a TV in the corner there, have a music centre here – there's even room to dance!'

Upstairs the gang had thrown open the bedroom doors, invaded the attic that stretched out under the whole roof and were busy arguing over which room would be better for boys and which for girls. Peter turfed them out to explore the outbuildings. There were certainly plenty of bedrooms, even allowing for turning two into bathrooms. Bathrooms! To be clean! Really clean!

'And we could easily turn the attic into a room or two, which would give us eight large rooms altogether.'

I fought to keep my excitement under control. The house felt so warm, so welcoming, so right.

'Let's check out the stables and the barn,' said Peter.

The gang raced up to us as we stepped out into the sun once more.

'We could have workshops in the stables!'

'We could learn to swim in the river!'

'There's space for a football pitch in the barn!'

'There's a cowshed where we could have a school of our own...'

'Hold on, hold on!' laughed Peter. 'It's not as easy as that! No point in having a schoolroom if you haven't got a teacher.'

'If you'll have me, I'll stay and be your teacher. Anna, the girl from the mission who works with me – she might take over,' said Tania shyly. 'This place is incredible – I just feel as if it's my home already. Would there be room for me?'

Peter smiled. 'I think we might fit you in somewhere.' For the first time that day, Maria's face relaxed and she smiled a warm smile of relief at Tania.

The doctor said, 'If you'll allow me, I could come out some weekends – maybe teach you how to play football properly?'

This suggestion was met with a roar of approval.

'But *we'll* teach *you* how to play football, Doctor!' shouted Chico.

'So,' said Peter, swallowing, 'shall we buy this farm and make it our home?'

'*Yes!*'

Peter took a step nearer the silent girl. 'Maria?'

Maria put her hands on her hips and looked down at the sun-baked ground. She spoke slowly.

'The gang need a home. This is so perfect; it must be a gift from God. You must buy it, Peter. They can grow up in peace and safety in this beautiful place. Everything is just as I would have wanted it for them. But...'

Peter's voice was very gentle. 'But what, Maria?'

'It is too far from the city for me. I cannot leave the city. It is the only place I will ever find out what happened to José, my brother. One day I will meet someone who can tell me what happened that night he disappeared. Perhaps when I find out I will be able to come here and live in peace with you. Until then, I must go back to the city and keep asking.'

Peter was about to speak when Tania made a sudden protective movement.

'Who's that?' she said. It was a sign of how on edge the gang still were, that without even looking, the younger ones whipped behind Maria and me to hide.

A gaunt figure was making his way across the yard from behind the stables. As he drew nearer, I felt my jaw drop in surprise. 'But that's Rodrigo!'

'The Rodrigo in the street fight? Who gave us a picnic? It can't be,' said Peter. 'Not all the way out here.'

But sure enough, Peter recognised him too – the boy we had rescued from the thugs all that time ago.

Chico ran to greet him and thumped him on the back in glee.

'Rodrigo! It *is* you!'

The boy was taken aback, then a smile of delight and relief spread across his face.

'Chico? Marco? Peter! But what are you doing here?'

'Buying the farm!' sang out Chico. 'And you?'

'You're buying *this* farm? But this is the farm I told you about. The one where I found myself, where I worked, where the farmer was put in prison for ill-treating us. There was no sign of my family in the city, so I had nowhere else to go. I came back, looking for work around here, in one of the villages perhaps, until I think of what to do next. And I find... you!'

I turned to Maria in delight. 'Remember? We told you about Rodrigo! The boy who lost his memory? This is him.'

But Maria had gone very pale. She stood as if she'd been turned to stone.

'Maria? He's our friend! Say something to him! Welcome him to the gang!'

'You're not Rodrigo,' she said at last, in a strangled voice. 'You're José. You're my brother. The one who disappeared.'

Rodrigo's blue-grey eyes locked on to Maria's.

'Maria?' he asked. 'My sister? I have a sister?' He stared at her, then went over to her, looking down into the eyes that were a mirror image of his own. Then his baffled frown turned to a blazing grin in a glorious moment of understanding. 'I had a sister. I *have* a sister. Of course! I remember now! How could I ever forget?' He fought for the memories, staring intently at Maria as if she could tell him everything. Then he spoke slowly. 'I had left you back in the tunnel with the little ones. I was down at the dump, collecting newspapers to sell for pulp. I turned to put an armload into the cart. Someone shouted, "The death squad van!" I dropped everything and ran, but there was a car – it ran into me. Then the next thing I knew, I was waking up in the stable there. With a headache.'

'The farmer knocked you down, panicked...' I thought out loud.

'Perhaps he thought he'd killed you and wanted to get your body out of sight,' added Chico.

'When you woke up with no memory, he must have thanked his lucky stars and set you to work for him here,' said Gilberto through gritted teeth.

Maria wasn't listening. Her eyes were on her brother.

'I looked after the gang, José,' whispered Maria. 'When you'd gone, I took care of them.'

'Maria,' he said. Then with a great shout of joy, he picked her up, and whirled her round, hugging her to him. 'My little sister!' The children who had been watching, wide-eyed, started to cheer and shout. Those who remembered José ran to him. Tania was staring at José, tears pouring down her face. Below the din the children were making, I could hear her quiet prayer, '*Thank you. Thank you. Thank you.*'

José was so instantly a part of the family, fitted so

perfectly into the circle of friends who jostled around him that I couldn't bear the thought that he might not want to stay with us. I tried to keep the anxiety out of my voice. 'You will stay with us here now, José?' I said.

'Try to stop me!' he laughed, his arms tight round Maria and Chico.

'I think,' said Peter, rubbing his eyes, 'this calls for a celebration picnic. Rodri... José! I owe you this!'

And Peter spread a huge rug out on the ground in the shade of the tree in the courtyard. Together we pulled the bags and boxes out of the bus. The gang fell on them, pulling out new bread, cheese, salami, ham, a crate of ripe peaches, bunches of grapes, huge slabs of chocolate and bottle after bottle of lemonade, fruit juice, wine and water, all devoured in a constant babble of excitement.

At last, when everybody's shouts and laughter and tears had died down to a contented hum, José raised a bottle and called for silence.

'Ladies and gentlemen, a toast. To the house we will soon call our home; to Senhor Peter who brought us to it, and to Maria, who kept you and your faith alive. Go with God.'

And the valley rang with claps, cheers and the answer that roared back,

'*Go with God!*'

Note from the author

The events in this story are completely fictional but the setting is based on real life. The street children of South America in the twenty-first century lead lives that are difficult, rough, deprived and dangerous.

My heartfelt thanks go to Sarah de Carvalho whose faith and work depicted in her book The Street Children of Brazil *inspired this story.*

If you would like to support the street children, you could contact Happy Child Mission, the charity Sarah and her husband have set up for this work by sending an email to happychild@wecc.org.uk

Or you could send a donation to:
Happy Child Mission
PO Box 628
28 Old Brompton Road
London
SW7 3SS